MOMS
IN THE
WILD

Celebrating
30 Years of Publishing
in India

MOMS
IN THE
WILD

NIDHI RAICHAND

HarperCollins *Publishers* India

First published in India by HarperCollins *Publishers* 2023
4th Floor, Tower A, Building No 10, DLF Cyber City,
DLF Phase II, Gurugram, Haryana – 122002
www.harpercollins.co.in

2 4 6 8 10 9 7 5 3 1

P-ISBN: 978-93-5629-385-4
E-ISBN: 978-93-5629-386-1

Typeset in 10.5/14 Utopia Std at
Manipal Technologies Limited, Manipal

Printed and bound at
Replika Press Pvt. Ltd.

To my cubs, Avi and Zoya.

CHAPTER 1

My first solo job as a reporter was to interview a dead woman.

To be fair to my editor, she never meant to assign me such an impossible task. After all, this was my first month as a full-time employee at the website Cactus, and I'd been put on the lifestyle beat, which was historically, a fairly straightforward section that involved people who sometimes had style but who always, *always*, had life. And at the time I was briefed, the woman in question was very much alive. The email assigning me the story still resides at the bottom of my inbox, one amongst the deluge of the usual first-month-of-work emails, which included a welcome mail, important links, instructions on reimbursements and a calendar invite to a session on women's safety at the workplace.

Natasha Babani is the president of the residents' association for Whispering Willows, a residential complex situated near Lake Ahilya. In less than six months as president, she has managed to mobilize residents of her community as well as others around the lake and initiate the much-needed

Clean Ahilya drive. Experts say that the levels of effluents have already drastically reduced, and Mrs Babani and her team's final aim is to make the lake free of toxins by the end of her presidency.

In her spare time, Mrs Babani loves to spend time with her husband and two adorable children, grow organic vegetables in her terrace garden and paint using natural colours. She's also a trained Pilates instructor and certified chartered accountant.

Sneha, please do a 500-word profile on this woman. Focus on the lake clean-up angle.

—V

V, of course, was my editor. She is usually known as Vij, which is short for Vijaya. You'd think Vij was short enough to sign off emails with, but as you grow in your career, you get busier and the first thing you must sacrifice is your full name. I personally hope to be an 'S' someday, but as things stand, I still have time to write my full name.

There it was! My first-ever assignment at my first-ever job.

Technically, I'd been on probation with them for six months, but I was a proper employee now—on their rolls, with a provident fund account and everything—and boy, was I going to make them glad they hired me! I was going to make this the best profile of a lake cleaning, terrace-garden growing, painter, Pilates instructor, chartered accountant, mother of two that the world had ever seen. It would be the profile that put all other profiles to shame. The one that would shine the spotlight on me and prove to the journalistic world that I was not just another millennial–Gen Z cusper, silly campus recruit but also an empathetic storyteller with an original voice and a special insight into her subjects. I pictured blue ticks on my Twitter and Instagram accounts, mentions in 30-under-30 lists and did I dare say it out loud—even a TedX talk.

But first, Natasha Babani. I painstakingly drafted an official (but friendly) email to her, in which I told her how fascinated I was with her story and requested an interview with her for our website. And as I awaited a response, I began my secondary research by turning to the world wide web to see what it had to say about this wonder woman.

Natasha Babani's online presence was like a big, bursting-with-life, technicolour version of the little profile she'd shared with us. She was indeed a Pilates instructor with a weakness for fun, little stories and high-energy reels of her students strengthening their cores. There were pictures of her beautiful apartment—all windows and white furniture— and if the artwork on the walls was hers, the woman really could weave magic with those natural paints. There were several pictures of her and her family on vacation, featuring her two boys wearing matching clothes and doing all sorts of adorable boy things, like splashing in the pool, hanging on their father's arms, kissing their mother's face and standing proudly next to a snowman (a *snowman*!). Her husband looked like an Indian Russell Crowe—all big and handsome and bear-like. And then there was Natasha.

Natasha was an absolute vision—tall and golden with a wavy bob, big brown eyes, a long lean, body and the biggest, cheekiest smile I'd ever seen. She had impeccable taste in clothes and a great flair for mixing and matching assorted styles and lengths of necklaces. I could've been doing a profile on her as an Instagram influencer; she had over 25,000 followers. Yet, here I was, waiting to interview her on how she'd cleaned up one of the most polluted lakes in the city. It really was too bad that she was dead.

CHAPTER 2

It's a funny thing—the death of someone you've never met but feel like you know intimately. A part of you is in mourning, and another part is puzzled and mildly judgemental of this unnecessary sentimentality you're feeling.

But you see, my acquaintance with Natasha Babani wasn't merely one-sided online stalking. In the days between our first correspondence and planned interview, Natasha and I had had several interactions. To my first email, she responded with enthusiasm; she was so thrilled about the profile. She couldn't wait to meet me and show me around the lake and tell me the story of the difference it had made to her and all her neighbours. She was terribly sorry she was in Thailand for the weekend but would be back soon. She was available on email and WhatsApp until then, happy to share any information that I might like about the Clean Ahilya drive. Could I please text her on WhatsApp so that she could save my number as well?

'*Hi, this is Sneha Talwar from Cactus,*' I texted her on WhatsApp, and received a reply a few seconds later.

'*Hey!!! So good to connect with you! Back in a couple of days. Catch you then.*'

Her display picture suggested that she was away on some sort of girls' trip. I responded saying I was looking forward to meeting her and wishing her fun in Thailand, figuring that was the end of our exchange.

But my phone beeped again—Natasha was still not done with this conversation, and she told me it was a friend's bachelorette trip. She was so happy that 'Putts' had found love again, and that she, Natasha, was her informal maid of honour.

Emboldened by her volunteering of this bit of personal information, I wondered if I ought to add her as a Facebook friend. But too soon, I decided. Perhaps I could do it after I finished the interview, which we scheduled for the coming Thursday afternoon.

As I waited patiently for Natasha to land back in India, I started my research on the lake, which was one of Bangalore's most famous lakes, located near the city centre. For decades, it had been just another natural landmark in the city surrounded by a frequently used jogging track and a children's park that was maintained around once in ten years. Some of the land around it seemed to be disputed, and there wasn't too much construction, barring a couple of office buildings and the posh 100-apartment Whispering Willows residential complex.

The residents of Whispering Willows had their own walking tracks (rubber and paved), a gym and three children's parks that were maintained on a daily basis. The only purpose Lake Ahilya served was as a reason to charge higher rents for the lake-facing apartments. And it wasn't until a little over a year ago, when the residents of these lake-facing apartments woke up one morning to the soothing smell of their filter coffee mixed with a horrifying stench from the lake, that folks began to notice that the lake was dying.

Without warning, thousands of dead fish had washed up on the banks of the Ahilya, and the residents of Whispering Willows were stupefied. How could this happen in one of the most high-end neighbourhoods in the city? That too just months after they had made garbage segregation compulsory in every home. What was in the lake water and was it also in their drinking water? Were their kids and families safe? And what was going to happen to the property prices in Whispering Willows?

It had been a frenzied week of meetings with the local authorities and private agencies to clean up the mess and fix whatever was ailing the lake. Thankfully, the water from the lake did not mix with Whispering Willows' water supply, but an investigation was deemed necessary, and the Bruhat Bengaluru Mahanagara Palike (BBMP) requested volunteers from Whispering Willows.

That had been the day that Natasha Babani, a concerned citizen with a flexible work schedule and two kids in school till 4 p.m., had vowed to stop sitting around and do something about whatever had caused that terrible fish massacre. Although she didn't know it then, cleaning up that lake would be her life's biggest accomplishment and also where she would unfortunately meet her sad end. It was a good thing the lake had been so clean when she drowned. She really did always hate a mess.

<h1 style="text-align:center">CHAPTER 3</h1>

It was a beautiful Tuesday morning in Bangalore as I sat scrolling through Instagram and came across a ton of pictures from Natasha's trip. The hashtag #YouOnlyLiveOnceButCanFindLoveTwice seemed to be the theme of the trip. In a couple of posts, she had made mistakes in spelling out that rather arduous hashtag, a slip I found terribly endearing. There were also pictures of her reuniting with her boys with the hashtags #NoPlaceLikeHome, #MamasBoys and #MomFirst. There was one picture of Bangalore taken from the aircraft as it was landing, hashtagged #GoodToBeHome.

I promptly sent her a text, warmly welcoming her back and asking when I could interview her. She texted back to say that she was going to be busy with the kids in the complex for the next few days and if late Thursday morning would work for me. Sure, I responded, and before I could ask, she sent me her address with a helpful location pin.

Busy with the building kids doing what *exactly*, I wondered. I scoured her Instagram feed over the next couple of days, but there were no updates apart from a picture of a kitten she'd found abandoned and was fostering until someone gave it a warm and loving home.

The tragedy that was about to unfold less than forty-eight hours later would leave several victims in its wake. The heartbroken husband and kids, of course. The largest group of 'close' friends I'd ever come across. The fragile ecosystem of Lake Ahilya that would sadly never be completely free of toxins. And that poor little kitten who never did get adopted and instead most likely strolled off to a violent fate.

CHAPTER 4

'*Madam phone nahi utha rahi hain,*' said the guard for the fourth time, code for 'Please step away from the gate; you're not going in.' This was Whispering Willows, and there was a five-step verification process you had to pass before you were to be allowed entry into its hallowed gates. The last and most important one was confirmation from the resident that they knew you and could vouch for your worthiness as a human being, and Natasha Babani was seriously letting me down right then. She was also ignoring my text messages and calls. Out of options and feeling more than a little desperate, I opened my email thread to see if there was some other way to reach her. That's when I noticed another name in the introductory email—Jaya Venkataraman, vice-president of the residents' association. And hurray, there was also a phone number.

One call, one frantic explanation and three minutes later, I was finally allowed through the grand entrance of Whispering Willows. Stepping in was like passing into another world. The place was overwhelmingly, breath-stoppingly, pristinely beautiful. Spread over several acres were five-storey buildings designed in an imposing yet cosy, colonial style, all-white columns and sloping red roofs. Wide alleys with lush landscaping divided the blocks, each named after a popular British tree. Discreet little boards poking out from behind flowering bushes pointed you to the clubhouse or the pool or the residents' welfare association office. This was like a high-end resort, and I couldn't believe people *lived* here on a daily basis.

As I walked towards the reception of the Maple block, where Jaya said she'd meet me, I quickly checked my phone to see what the rents here were like. Hmm, yeah—maybe if ten of us got together to stay in a three-bedroom ...

'Hi! Are you Sneha?' I heard a friendly voice ask, and I looked up from my phone to see a young woman in a white cotton sleeveless dress and strappy leather chappals walking towards me. As I tucked my phone in my bag and nodded, she stuck out her hand and smiled. 'Jaya. It's lovely to meet you. So sorry about all this confusion.'

'No worries at all, Jaya. Thanks for coming to my rescue,' I replied, feeling completely out of place and overdressed in my stupid black trousers, white formal shirt and expensive blue Zara blazer I'd bought like I was going to be a political correspondent at the White House. Whispering Willows was made for expensive resort wear crafted from natural fabrics in the colours of the countryside (British, not Indian).

'Come, let's go to the RWA office and I'll try and figure out where Natasha is,' Jaya said, beckoning me down another exquisitely landscaped pathway. 'It's totally unlike her to miss an appointment. She's usually extremely organized and punctual.'

'That's okay. She's probably just stuck somewhere. I'm happy to wait,' I shouted over the click-clacking of my stupid new formal heels that were studiously sawing through my ankles with every step I took on the stone pathway.

'Yeah, but I can't get through to her phone, and she's not responding to my texts, which is *extremely* unusual,' said Jaya. 'Hang on, I'll ask Babu if he's seen her.'

Babu, who I assumed was their accountant, had also not seen Natasha and added that she'd missed the finance meeting that had been scheduled for earlier that morning.

'Hain!' said Jaya. 'Where could she be? Do you mind if we go check her apartment? I'm so sorry about this, Sneha.'

Sorry? About taking me to only the most beautifully decorated apartment in the most luxe condominiums ever made in Bangalore? Natasha Babani's tardiness was going to give me enough fodder to entertain friends and family for the next six months. But I had to be cautious not to appear overenthusiastic, and so I muttered a soft 'No problem,' nodded vaguely and followed Jaya down another cobbled path, this time to the Elm block.

Through another tastefully done building lobby and into the lift we went. Jaya pressed '4' on the lift panel—the penthouse, of course—and gave me a friendly smile as the shiny lift doors closed and our own watery reflections appeared in them.

'So, have you lived here long?' I asked conversationally. The lift was too intimate a space and travelling in silence was going to be impossible.

'Um, actually my family has been here for a few years. I just moved back in with them a few months ago,' Jaya said. 'I was studying abroad and then working,' she added helpfully. 'So umm ... yeah.'

The lift came to a smooth halt and we stepped out into a warmly lit corridor, right outside Natasha's apartment. A couple of plants, a shiny lion's head knocker and a slim nameplate with 'Babanis' embossed on it confirmed we were at the right place. Jaya rang the doorbell, and seconds later, a youngish woman's face peeked out from behind the door. As her eyes went from my face to Jaya's, her expression changed from suspicious to friendly.

'Jaya Didi,' she said with a smile and opened the door completely.

'Hi, Mary,' Jaya said. 'Is Natasha home?'

'Natasha Didi not there since morning, didi,' Mary replied. 'She is dropping the children to the bus stop and then going for walk, she said, didi.'

'That must've been at, like, seven-something in the morning,' wondered Jaya, her brow furrowed in concern and confusion. 'She couldn't still be out walking ...'

I was concerned too but about not being able to see into the house. Mary seemed to be standing in some sort of entrance vestibule, and all I could see were parts of a console and a very stylish, modern, bevelled mirror. It was like one mirror made up of multiple mirrors—very interiors meets engineering—and it reflected nothing but the front door.

Damn these wealthy apartments and their privacy features! The front door of the apartment my roommate and I shared opened straight into our living room and you could see into our kitchen, both our bedrooms and the rear balcony if you opened it just a crack. Fortunately, we had nothing to hide but one large sofa and a wicker bookshelf that held five books and a precariously balanced modem and router.

'Should we do that then, Sneha?'

My concentrated effort to peek into Natasha's apartment was suddenly broken. 'Sorry, what? I was just ... um ... fascinated by this mirror,' I muttered.

'Yeah, I know, it's gorgeous. You should see the rest of Natasha's house. I just love her taste in bloody everything—she's so talented!' Jaya responded enthusiastically. 'So I was thinking that maybe she's waiting by the lake for you—should we check there?'

'Absolutely,' I agreed. 'Let's go walk by the lake.' I looked down mournfully at my heels that were not meant for walking by the lake or anywhere on this planet.

Sometimes, great friendships are based on great pain, and for Jaya and me, outwardly two of the unlikeliest people to ever form a bond, it was my very stylish but very painful shoes that converted a chance meeting into one of my closest relationships.

'Those things giving you a shoe bite?' she asked. 'Let's stop off at my place, and I'll give you a pair of flats to wear.'

I protested weakly as we entered the lift but Jaya saw right through me, and minutes later, I was seated on a bench outside Jaya's block as she came through, triumphantly brandishing a white Magnolia Bakery bag with a pair of black flip-flops.

'Here you go,' she said, smiling. 'You can change back into your heels when you see Natasha and conduct your interview.'

'Hehe, yeah,' I said, gratefully swapping the ankle killers for the flip-flops. 'That was the first thing they taught us in journalism school, to always be wearing stylish shoes when interviewing your subject.'

With a swing in my step and a new-found camaraderie, I followed Jaya down one of those charming stone paths, round the housing blocks, past rows of colourful bougainvillea playfully covering what appeared to be the complex's water filtration plant, towards a little gate almost invisible amongst the greenery and the white compound wall. That was Whispering Willows' exclusive secret side entrance to Lake Ahilya, saving its residents the several steps and the hassle of having to cross the main road.

It was nearly noon now, and the 40-hectare lake was mostly deserted. We were at the south end, which had a well-maintained stone bank, a wide walking path and a couple of benches helpfully placed under trees. Jaya looked around to see if she could spot Natasha, and I walked towards the water to see just how clean it was.

'Well, she's not here,' said Jaya. 'I really can't imagine what's up with her. I'm going to try her phone once again—this is so weird because she's so proud of the work she's done on this lake, you know. I mean, by the time I moved here, the smell issues had already been sorted out, but she didn't stop at just that. She was really committed to, like, making it the cleanest lake in the country or something. Nope, still can't get through. Damn, when technology lets you down, I swear it's so frustrating ...'

Jaya had walked towards me as she was talking and suddenly stopped mid-sentence as her eyes landed upon what I had been staring at for a few seconds. A few feet below the surface of the water was bobbing what was clearly the outline of a woman in a white T-shirt and dark bottoms. The body seemed to be floating up to the surface, but something was holding her left arm down. While I couldn't see the face, I was pretty sure who this was, except that I was unable to get a word out and stood there in silent shock for what seemed like hours.

Jaya, however, had the opposite reaction.

'Oh my god! Oh fuck. Fuck! Fuck! *Natasha*. Fuck, that's Natasha! Oh fuck. Fuck!'

CHAPTER 5

There was an ambulance. And people—lots and lots of people. There were some security guards, some Whispering Willows residents, including Jaya's parents, a bunch of police officers and many others whose origins I couldn't quite place. At some point, in this crowd of complete strangers, I spotted a couple of familiar faces—Vijaya, my editor, had sent in two senior colleagues to rescue me from what she rightly surmised was a situation I was not equipped to handle.

Natasha's body was retrieved from the water. Apparently, her hand had been sucked into the vent of some sort of filtration mechanism in the side of the lake. I couldn't quite understand the details, and nobody was bothering to explain. Jaya and I were asked to go and wait at the clubhouse, and as we were herded from one point to another, I passed a tall, distraught-looking man who looked vaguely familiar. People were asking us questions, and other people were telling those people to step aside and give us some space. On three different occasions, the cops asked us to recount what we'd seen and how we'd come upon the body. There was talk of us having to go to the police station, but we eventually didn't end up going.

It was late evening when I was finally able to find my way back to the office. Barring one or two, most people had left for the day. Cactus wasn't an organization that encouraged working late, and Vijaya was always out of the building by 5 p.m. But today, the light in her corner office was still on, and just as I was passing by, the door opened and she asked me to come in.

'Hi, Vij,' I said softly as I went inside and flumped myself into a chair.

'Sneha! We send you to cover a story, and you *become* the story. That's not something journalists are encouraged to do, haha!' Vijaya said, trying an empathetic but light-hearted approach. It was kind yet strange; I'd only known Vijaya as someone who talked business and kept the joshing around to a minimum.

She did, however, seem genuinely concerned. 'Coming across a dead body like that must have been traumatic, Sneha. You told me your family lives in Chandigarh, right? We can arrange for you to go home for some time. You don't have to worry about leave or getting there ...'

'No, no, there's no need for that,' I interrupted. The thought of going home was infinitely less appealing than being here. 'I want to continue working and find out what happened. I'll be fine—I share an apartment with my best friend, and I have a ton of other friends here, and my parents' friends' place is there in case I need to go see them.'

'Hmm, you feel like this now, but the shock can sink in at any time. You have to let us know any time you're starting to feel uneasy, okay?'

'Yes, I'll do that for sure. Thanks, Vij. I actually didn't see much, you know. I mean, I saw the body in the water, and then, by the time they pulled her out, so many people had gathered and the cops were there—I didn't feel like pushing through the crowd and seeing her up close.'

'Oh god.' Vijaya grimaced, clearly more upset than I'd thought. 'I'm so sorry your first assignment turned out like this, Sneha. Come, shall we get you home now? Where do you live?'

I assured Vijaya that I didn't live too far away and that I had my trusty two-wheeler to take me home. I could tell that she wanted to do something, help me out in some way, but honestly, I wasn't feeling as shaken up as I imagine she thought I was. What had happened was horrible and macabre and unbelievable but at the same time really exciting!

Oh god, what was wrong with me? Why did I feel this was exciting? I had stumbled upon a *dead body*. In all the journalism courses I'd taken and all the stories I'd heard from my seniors, there were none that began with, 'In case you go to interview someone and they turn up dead, here's what you do ...'

I went to use the restroom, splashed some water on my face and came back to pick up my things before going with Vijaya to the parking lot. As we walked down the stairs, she smiled at me and said, 'In the mood for some banana pudding tonight? You've earned it.'

'Huh?' I asked, not quite understanding.

'Your Magnolia Bakery bag,' Vijaya said, raising her eyebrows at my hand. 'I love their banana pudding.'

'Oh, these,' I said, suddenly remembering the great shoe exchange I'd participated in earlier that day. With everything that followed, I'd obviously forgotten to return Jaya's shoes and had been lugging this bag around with me everywhere all day. And now it meant that at some point, I needed to go back to Whispering Willows to return them.

This was clearly not over.

CHAPTER 6

Friday morning—not yet twenty-four hours since our ill-fated meeting that never really came to fruition. My first call was from the police station, asking me to come in and tell them my account of what had happened again. Vijaya had asked me to take the day off, but I texted to update her about this development while turning down her offer for someone to accompany me. My next text was to Jaya, who hadn't been called to the cop station yet and said sure, I could come by any time to drop off her shoes, she was home all day.

Plenty of waiting, form-filling, photocopying, signing and talking later, I was back at the scene of the crime. Ha! No pun intended, I thought, as I parked my little two-wheeler outside Whispering Willows and went through the guest sign-in process. As I walked to Jaya's block, I thought about how the place was still as overwhelmingly beautiful as when I'd first seen it, but the sense of peace was now entirely missing. Was I feeling this way because of what had happened, or did it have anything to do, I wondered, with the gaggle of women who had taken over the lawns outside Elm, the block where Natasha Babani lived. Had lived.

I didn't want to stare, but it was impossible not to be captivated by this particular group of ladies. They were like an Instagram post—#TastefulMourning, #BeautyInDeath, #ShadesOfAFuneral. Women of all shapes and sizes, mostly wearing shades of white and off-white with perhaps a bit of denim here or a flash of indigo there. They were nearly all impeccably turned out, and I was hard-pressed to find one perfectly coloured head of hair that didn't have a pair of designer sunglasses perched on it. There must've been at least twenty of them, scattered in groups of three or four. Some were speaking in hushed tones, and some were just standing around with quietly sympathetic expressions.

'Hey.' It was a tired voice from the other direction, and I turned to see Jaya waving at me from inside her block's reception. She was looking very thin and extremely exhausted, like someone who hadn't slept much and just wanted this to be over.

'Hey, Jaya,' I said quietly. 'How're you doing?'

'Oh god, not great at all. I'm in some sort of shock or disbelief, I think. God knows what bloody stage of mourning, or whatever the hell one feels after discovering a friend's goddamn dead body, this is. Hey, thanks,' she said as she reached to take her flip-flops and guided me to a sofa in the reception.

'I'm trying to avoid the bloody assembly of mourning mothers out there. I *cannot* take another person wanting to hear how it happened but "only if I'm up to it", she said, using air quotes. 'And then giving me shit advice and completely unsolicited hugs. Ugh!'

'*All* those women are Natasha's friends?'

'Oh, they're just the tip of the iceberg! Dude, Natasha was the most popular woman in Bangalore city. Fuck, I still can't believe she's dead. And like that ...' Jaya shook her head, looking so tired and distraught that I started to feel guilty about my own underreaction to this whole thing. Perhaps it was just delayed, I figured. Some sort of fight-or-flight thing my brain was doing to protect me from trauma, I thought, not quite believing my own weak arguments based on pop psychology picked up mostly from BuzzFeed quizzes.

Not sure what the appropriate thing to say or do was, I awkwardly patted Jaya's shoulder a couple of times. It was just dawning on me that I shared what was probably the most momentous, and certainly the most bizarre, thing to happen to me with a woman I didn't know at all. Unfortunately, I hadn't yet come across a BuzzFeed quiz that gave me options on what to do next.

It's the day after you and a total stranger, whose footwear you've just borrowed, come across the dead body of a woman whom you didn't know at all and whom she knew very well. Do you:

a.   *Hug each other for thirty seconds or more*
b.   *Look up the number for a therapist who does joint trauma therapy*
c.   *Ask the stranger if she will be promoted to president of her residents' association now that the original president is dead*
d.   *Sit quietly in the stranger's plush reception lobby and keep your mouth shut because this whole thing is just too unreal*

D! D! I was both picking D and giving myself a pass for not knowing what the hell to do in this situation. I was clearly out of my depth here, but the fact that I had managed to shower, go to the police station and now sit here with the presence of mind to awkwardly pat Jaya on the shoulder meant that I was doing okay.

Jaya turned and looked at me, her eyes wide. 'I'm sorry for sounding bitchy, but, dude, these women, these so-called friends of Natasha? They can be fierce. And I don't mean a good, Beyonce kinda fierce—they're borderline frightening. I don't know, ya—maybe it has to do with being moms. Brings out the inner lionesses in them or something.'

'How do you know they're all moms?' I asked, slightly put-off by this rather pigeon-holey, non-feminist description of the women.

'Oh, being a mom was Natasha's jam. I think this lake clean-up was the first thing she'd done that didn't revolve around her kids or their school or didn't directly involve her other mom friends,' said Jaya.

'I moved here nearly a year ago,' she continued. 'And, boy, have I gotten to see these mothers up close. They're ... *intense*. You should do a story about them!' she said, laughing.

I smiled back. 'Yeah, because I'm sure there are absolutely *no* websites or books or blogs dedicated only to mothers!'

'No, but that content is generated by them, about them. To quote my old boss whom I worked with only for six months before I ran away, all those mommy publications take an inside-out approach. We need to take an outside-in approach, see?'

'Ah! So I'd be like a Nat Geo wildlife filmmaker, with my telephoto zoom lens camera, watching and recording the animals in their natural habitat from afar and then getting a famous British actor to record my findings for the final voice-over?'

'Exactly!' Jaya chuckled in delight. 'I mean, without the camera and the British actor and all, but the animals in their natural habitat sounds about right.'

I raised my arms and created a mock marquee over an imaginary movie theatre. 'Nat Geo showed you their mating rituals,' I said in my best announcer voice. 'We'll show you what happens after the babies are born, are slightly grown up and are in school and all that!'

'*Mothers in the Wild*—a Sneha and Jaya production!'

At this point, both of us dissolved into giggles, not so much because any of what we'd said was especially witty or clever but because it was the first bit of relief in what had been a very tense twenty-four hours. The human spirit is resilient like that, I suppose.

CHAPTER 7

Chatting with Jaya was nice. She had an easy, relaxed manner, and she was not shy to air an outrageous or completely inappropriate thought from time to time. She'd quit her boring job and insufferable boss in Gurgaon (her words, not mine) because she'd gotten into her dream master's programme in education policy at the George Washington University. She had decided to spend a couple of months with her parents before heading off to the US. That's how she'd moved back to Bangalore after having been away for several years of studying and working.

She'd grown up in a big bungalow in JP Nagar, which, according to her, was a different planet from Whispering Willows. But her parents had grown tired of living in and maintaining the place, especially after both the kids had left, and they had decided to sell and move to a nice, airy apartment, which was also closer to where her mother's family lived. They were thrilled to have their daughter come home after so long, and Jaya was happy to bum around and discover a new part of the city she had grown up in.

Then, just a month before she was due to leave for her graduate programme, Jaya had met with a car accident. It was a bad accident, and she'd been seriously hurt. She had ended up in hospital for three weeks and had come home just in time to defer her admission by a year. She'd then begun a long process of recovery and rehabilitation, which included daily physiotherapy and occupational therapy.

Jaya had been determined to work on getting better quickly and had worked hard with her therapists. Soon, she was able to get around on her own, and that's when she'd met and befriended Natasha Babani.

'I'd started walking in the compound with my walking stick, and one day, I'd decided to take a round of the children's play area. I remember it was super loud and noisy with all these kids running and jumping around. Most of the kids had their nannies with them, sitting on the benches with water bottles and snack boxes, occasionally shouting to the kids not to fight or give some other child a turn on the slide.

'There was only one mom there, and she wasn't sitting on the side—she was standing next to the monkey bars and loudly cheering for her sons. I noticed her immediately. She was wearing something simple, in beige and brown or something, but she was so tall and beautiful that she'd stand out anywhere.'

Jaya's voice became softer as she continued, 'She was really sweet, ya. She saw me hobbling about, came up to me and just started chatting. This was the first time we'd met, but she was so unselfconscious and warm—by the end of our chat, we'd exchanged numbers. She even sent me a WhatsApp that night, just saying good night, hoping I was feeling better after my walk, you know.'

A text to say good night? To someone you've just met? Were we in twenty-first-century Bangalore or in a fictional children's book about the importance of being nice? Jaya saw the look on my face and jumped in to explain further.

'No, no!' she said. 'She wasn't a weirdo or anything. She was just a genuinely friendly person. You know how sometimes you feel like reaching out to someone but hold back because you don't want to come on too strong? The truth is, when you receive such kindness, it feels really special. And she was like this with everyone. I don't know how, but she found the time to stay in constant touch with everyone.

'She became my first real friend in Whispering Willows and pretty much lobbied to make me the vice-president of the association. Not like anyone else was dying to do the job—it's mostly just maintaining minutes of meetings and doing whatever the president tells you to do. But I had a whole year of nothing else to do, and I was honestly so taken by Natasha that I was just happy to hang out with her.'

Jaya became quiet and seemed lost in her thoughts for a few moments. Then she shook her head slowly, as if snapping herself out of her reverie. 'Shit, man, Natasha Babani is *dead*. I can't—I cannot, like, come to terms with it. I just *can't*.'

We sat there quietly, both lost in thought about the same person but in completely separate ways. Jaya knew her intimately and was mourning the loss of a close friend. I had never even met her and was feeling cheated at having been robbed of the opportunity of getting to know her. *I should continue working on that profile on her for the website*, I thought. Her death didn't diminish the work she'd done on cleaning the lake. And true, she was no celebrity one could do a full-blown obituary on, but she still sounded like a remarkable human being, one who had possibly touched more lives than any celebrity. Yup, that's how I was going to pitch this story to Vijaya—first thing at our next Monday editorial meeting. I could see it under the green-and-black masthead of the website—*The Legacy of an Ordinary Woman*. By Sneha Talwar. 4.2K retweets, 3,000 comments. Oh man, it was going to be wild.

I squeezed Jaya's shoulder—my go-to move to express grief and sympathy apparently—and got up. 'Hey, you take care now. Hope the police station isn't too much of an ordeal.' And then, inspired by Natasha and her policy of friendliness, I added, 'Let's stay in touch. Maybe we could hang out or something.'

Jaya got up and hugged me. 'Yup, I'd like that, Sneha. I'll catch you soon, okay!'

***

'OK, sorry in advance. I know this is TMI, but I thought you'd like to know. NB died of drowning because her hand got sucked into a suction duct or something and she couldn't pull it out. So, so awful. Can't stop thinking about it.☹️😔*'*

I cursed myself for breaking my vow of not looking at my phone first thing in the morning—a vow that had lasted one day and eleven minutes, but one that I could plainly see the wisdom in. There's only so much gory detail a cub reporter who has pretty much planned on only doing uplifting feature stories as a career plan can take.

Emoji or gif—what was the best way to respond? Words and an emoji, I decided. *'Shit, Jaya. That's horrible!!!!!! Can't even imagine her last moments. I'm shook.*💀*'*

Jaya texted back, '☹ *I have no words.*'

A few seconds later she pinged again. '*I think cops are releasing her body today. They'll probably do the cremation later. Can't deal but will go. Feel so bad for her poor family. Fuck.*'

For one second, I wondered if I should go for the cremation. No, I decided. That would be too much. '*You take care, babe* ☺,' I replied.

'*Will do. Bye.*'

CHAPTER 8

I spent the first half hour at work on Monday receiving hugs, soft shoulder pats (others do it too!) and several 'You okay, babes?' I almost felt guilty about actually being okay. The delayed shock I was expecting over the weekend had still not arrived, and I now needed to confront the possibility that I was a sociopath, incapable of feeling emotion even when confronted by a goddamn real, live dead body! Yes, *yes, I see what's wrong with that sentence but I'm a reporter, not an editor.*

And besides, I had other things to do now that our weekly edit meeting was beginning. My usual approach to these meetings was to go to the conference room with a pad, pen and cup of coffee, find a chair towards the far end of the long, rectangular table and wheel it back by just a few inches so that while my body was visible, my face was hidden behind a more seasoned member of staff. I was simply not confident enough to pitch stories, and I absolutely hated it when someone would seek me out to ask, 'So, what are you young people up to these days? We could mine *that* for a story.'

Young people are doing what all young people have ever done. Trying to earn money, get laid and dodge their worried mothers' calls.

The first time I was asked what my generation was up to, I facetiously said, 'Trying to be influencers.' I then spent the next two days researching and creating a listicle on Bangalore's top fitness and food influencers. It was not fun, and not just because my Instagram algorithm was now permanently broken and only showed people either flexing or stirring, but also because I did not want to be buried in fluffy listicle land. I was lazy but ambitious. I wanted to do features. And after the influencers incident, my policy was to keep my mouth shut and wait for something to be assigned to me.

Today, however, was different. Today, I *did* have a story to pitch. I made sure to sit up front where Vij and our deputy editor, Sahil, could see me. The posthumous profile of a nobody (the headline for this one just wrote itself)—this could be tricky, and I prepared myself for rejection. After the bulk of the agenda was discussed, Sahil opened the table to suggestions and story ideas, and even as a senior reporter started talking, I raised my hand.

'Sneha, I appreciate the enthusiasm, but you don't have to raise your hand,' Sahil said, smiling at me. 'We'll go around the table and come to you for sure.'

I waited another fifteen excruciating minutes as people droned on about garbage segregation, the land mafia and some local kid who'd been accepted into an Ivy League school on a full scholarship. How was any of this *still* news? Hadn't we known forever that landfills were going to kill the planet, that the land mafia would probably survive the first wave of deaths and that nerdy kids getting into fancy schools was a bedtime story all Indian children heard?

Finally, it was my turn, and putting on my best presentation voice, I turned to Vijaya. 'I want to do a posthumous report on Natasha Babani and all the good she did and all the lives she touched. I know she wasn't, like, well-known around the city or anything, but she really made an impact on that lake, and she was quite the celebrity within her community, which, by the way, is massive. I think it could be an inspiring story. Also, it would mean so much to her fam—'

Vijaya cut me off, saying, 'Sure, Sneha, you may work on the profile. Share timelines with Sahil after this meeting.'

And just like that, I was back in, doing a story on Natasha and her fascinating little world. One that was more exotic and unknown to me than the garbage, land and education mafias put together.

First step, though—get in touch with Jaya.

'So you'll give me all the information you have about the Clean Ahilya drive? Plus, I'll need a little bit about how she was as a person and as president of the association. And I'll also need you to hook me up with a bunch of her close friends so that I can write a more in-depth profile.'

'Hmm ...' Jaya was frowning. 'That's where we're going to have trouble. A list of her closest friends will run into several pages. I'm wondering how to whittle it down to just a few.'

Jaya and I were sitting in Jaya's drawing room—well, technically, her parents' drawing room. Her physiotherapy session had run late, and she had apologetically asked if I could come up and wait for a few minutes. Exactly as I'd assumed about all the other homes in the community, hers was also large and airy, and reeked of wealth. The furniture, paintings and other decorations were of an antique Chettinad style—lots of heavy teak sofas with ornate carvings, rich Tanjore paintings, brass statuettes and hanging diyas. It wasn't my personal style, but it certainly was classily done.

'You know,' I said, 'when Natasha and I were chatting before the interview, she'd mentioned some friend called Putts for whom she'd organized a bachelorette trip to Thailand. Maybe we could start there? She's probably tagged in her photos on Instagram. I could find out her full name.'

'Oh, I know Putts! Her full name is Premanjali Bhat. Don't look at me like that—I have no idea how Premanjali became Putts! But yeah, you could start there. She lives not too far away. I'll give you her number, and I'll text her saying you'll be calling?'

'Yes, please. That would be most helpful.'

'You know, I didn't realize Putts and Natasha were close. But like I said, I'd only known Natasha a few months—it's not like I knew *everything* about her.'

'Sure, but let's start with what you did know about her.' I placed my writing pad and a pen on the table and turned on my phone recorder. 'Mind if I record this?'

'Not at all,' said Jaya with a smile. 'Where should we begin? What do you want to know?'

'Let's start with the Clean Ahilya drive. How did she get involved?'

'She started the drive! Remember how a bunch of dead fish turned up on the banks of the lake one morning and everybody was horrified at what had happened? It was such a disturbing sight, and the smell was next-level putrid. Initially, the then-president of the RWA called the authorities, and I think they even got the local MLA to take a look. These guys cleared up the whole thing and promised it would never happen again, but Natasha wasn't satisfied with merely a clean-up. She wanted to know what had happened and how to prevent it from ever happening again. She got Varun Burman, a fellow at the Nehru Trust for Environmental Research, to come and take a sample and give us a full report. It seems that there were very high levels of ammonia in the water, which is highly toxic for fish.'

'How did the ammonia enter the lake?'

'Untreated sewage, evidently. The ammonia, along with lower-than-normal levels of dissolved oxygen and a particularly warm morning, contributed to the fish genocide—or pesce-cide, if there's such a word.'

Jaya continued, 'Natasha personally paid for the water study, and she made sure it got printed in the papers—I'll send you the links. By then, some other citizen groups found out about her efforts, and a lot of residents from Whispering Willows and the surrounding neighbourhoods joined her. That's how they created the Clean Ahilya drive. By the time I joined the association, the group was already working in high gear. They'd raised money and gotten in touch with environmental agencies to keep the water clean, and they were working with the civic authorities to install a sewage treatment plant for the lake. That's a huge project and would've taken a few years, but Natasha was determined to get it done.'

I was in awe. The task Natasha had taken on was by no means small or easy. 'And this was around the same time she became president of the residents' association?' I asked.

'What can I say? She was a real overachiever. She had this endless reservoir of energy. Must have been all those Pilates classes she took. People used to tease her that just hearing about her day would tire them out. I guess she could be pretty formidable that way.'

Something about the way Jaya said it made me look up from the frenetic note-taking. Was that a note of annoyance in her voice? Or was it something else? Whatever it was, it didn't sound very complimentary. Her face, however, didn't reveal any negativity. She still had a soft smile on her face, and her eyes had that slightly faraway look of someone recalling details from the past. I shook my head. I must've misunderstood.

We chatted for another twenty minutes, and I got more details about the Clean Ahilya drive as well as Natasha's duties as association president. It was time to head back to the office. I took Putts', number, thanked Jaya for her time and the filter coffee, and made my way out.

I started recapping all the adjectives about Natasha I'd heard so far—driven, energetic, friendly, overachiever. And now formidable. She sure was one multifaceted woman.

CHAPTER 9

People to interview

Friends: Five to six
Association accountant, Babu: One quote would be good
Old work colleague: Maybe?
Clean Ahilya drive members: One to two
Husband: Definitely (ugh, not looking fwd)
Anyone else?

My little profile on an unknown environmental do-gooder was getting a little out of hand. Sahil, the deputy editor, certainly thought so and was ready to slash my list by half. I had to beg him to let me do this, promise that I would not take too long and assure him that I would be continuing work on all my other assignments. Finally, I had to remind him that I'd discovered the woman's dead body. The last was an exceptionally cheap shot, and I could already tell by the withering look he gave me that within five minutes of my leaving his desk, there was going to be a #FuckingGenZ tweet from him. Ah well, as long as it got him to let me do what I wanted, my generation could take one for me.

In the few days between our last conversation and now, Jaya and I had connected several times over the phone and managed to make a slightly more substantial list of Natasha's friends to speak with. I enjoyed chatting with her, and she was generous with her appreciation of my jokes and funny observations. I had set up an interview with two of Natasha's very close friends for later that afternoon, and had promised to take Jaya out for coffee after to thank her for all her help. Meanwhile, Smita Dandekar and Sana Hussain would be waiting for me at 3 p.m. at Smita's house in Whispering Willows.

This would be my third visit to the complex in a week, and I was really starting to feel quite at home there. I'd dressed carefully that morning: boyfriend jeans folded at the bottom, my cute tan loafers and a white shirt with the old French tuck treatment—tucked in the front and left out at the back. I still may not have looked like a resident, but I certainly wouldn't stand out like a sore thumb either.

At 2.45 p.m. I was at the gate, by 2.50 p.m. my immigration formalities were complete and by 2.55 p.m. I was being escorted by Smita's domestic help from the front door to the drawing room.

As I followed her, I wondered if I had just stepped into someone's home or a hotel lobby. I had arrived in the hometown of brown and beige and every shade they had birthed between them. The marble floors were a shiny beige. The curtains were beige.

The sofa—an enormous sectional in beige—had matching shiny brown tables and brown velvet cushions.

Gatecrashing this brown–beige party were two wing chairs in a dull orange placed across from the long glass coffee table. Massive artworks adorned the walls—there was a red, orange and yellow abstract depicting masticating cows; a woman with a lotus and a bansuri, also in shades of orange; and finally, some sort of cubist dream in warm off-whites and browns with a big splash of red.

A squat little vase of fresh flowers, three fat coffee-table books—*Chanel, St Tropez Soleil* (orange cover!) and *A Princess Remembers*—and a dull gold tray with coasters and other knick-knacks were placed perfectly equidistant from each other on top of the coffee table. Right above it was one of those modern light installations with exposed bulbs, copper fittings and a bit of thick rope that had absolutely no purpose. Also thrown in with the furniture were a couple of brown leather pouffes—super cute but possibly not comfortable to sit on for more than a few minutes.

Ever ready to pass judgement, I immediately deemed this home the perfect love child of a family with lots of money but no taste and an interior designer who'd managed to build an entire career on the one creative idea they'd ever had.

I sat gingerly on one of the orange armchairs and pulled out my pad, pen and phone to get ready for the interview. A few minutes later, the girl who'd opened the door came back to offer me a glass of water and inform me that 'Madam' was just coming.

It would be many such 'waits' in drawing rooms, office lobbies and coffee shops later that I would come to understand that this trait of never greeting someone at the door yourself *and* keeping them waiting, even though they had arrived at a mutually agreed-upon time, was a special trait of the wealthy. It was an old trick to try and establish a power dynamic between yourself and your visitor and to send out the signal of 'busyness', that most important of all Indian virtues. Of course, all it really does is clearly announce to your visitor that you're an asshole and should be treated as one.

Finally, after making me wait for nearly ten minutes, Smita Dandekar came down her beige marble stairs and greeted me with a 'Hi, hi, hi!' and an apology (both equally tepid and fake). She was wearing leggings and a voluminous yellow kurta that seemed to envelop her like a meringue as she sank into her sofa.

'Sana will join us in a bit. Should we get started in the meantime?' she asked.

'Sure. Oh, and just so you know, I'll be taking notes and recording the interview as well so that I don't miss anything,' I replied. 'So, as Jaya may have told you, I was—'

'*Gayatri*!' bellowed Smita suddenly, startling me and causing the poor domestic worker to come running from the kitchen.

'Gayatri, bring my phone from upstairs, please. It should be at my desk—I think.'

As Gayatri scurried upstairs to get her phone, Smita looked at me apologetically and explained that her son's school bus would be arriving soon, and she needed to track it via the app.

'I mean, I've sent the nanny to pick him up from the gate, but I'd still like to know exactly where the bus is and at what time it arrives, you know. There are such creepies out there—things are just not how they were when we were kids.'

When *we* were kids? I'm twenty-four. And you're ... *not* twenty-four.

'Sure, yeah, I get it,' I said with a tight smile. 'So, as Jaya must've told you, I'm doing a story on Natasha Babani because she'd done so much for Ahilya Lake, and she also had quite an influence over everyone around her. I understand you guys were close.'

'*Were* close,' Smita said, catching her breath in what seemed to be her first genuine emotion of the day. 'I hate that I have to use the past tense for her. Natasha and I were like sisters. Her boys and my Aahan are the same age. We went through our pregnancies together, gave birth two months apart and have been really close ever since. We've taken our kids to extracurricular classes together—to birthday parties and holidays. I can't imagine a life without her, honestly ... Just a minute.'

Gayatri had arrived with Smita's phone, and she was now swiping it for what I assume were the bus's whereabouts.

'It's running a few minutes late. The traffic in this city, I tell you, it's getting worse day by day.'

'Are your son and Natasha's kids in the same school?'

'Umm ... no. Her boys go to Clearwood Academy. Vikram, their father, went there and was adamant they go there too. We wanted Aahan to do a more modern, progressive board, so we put him in Orion World School. I mean, both schools are really good, and the boys still play and go swimming together, and it's really not made much of a difference. We're very happy with Orion, you know—best decision we made for Aahan, even though it does cost twice as much as Clearwood, but then the IB board is known to be expensive. I just love their holistic approach to education. You know how we were asked to mug up everything and just reproduce? Well, the IB is different. It's much more inquiry-based—*and* they tackle topics that we weren't even aware of as kids.'

What on earth was happening? Why was I getting a lecture on a school curriculum? And why did she keep referring to herself and me as if we were part of some common subset? If she was close to Natasha's age, that made her at *least* fifteen years older than me. Also, I had no idea which school she'd gone to and what sort of education she'd had, but she had definitely not gone to the same boarding school as I had. And coming back to my first question—what was happening? Why was she going on about her child's school?

'So, uh, you've known Natasha how long then?'

'Oh, we met in our gynaecologist's waiting room when we were both pregnant, so that was, like, twelve years ago. We hit it off instantly, then we joined the same prenatal aerobics class, then our husbands got to know each other and that was *it*! I knew I'd met a friend for life. We all went to Goa when our kids were eight and ten months old respectively, and Natasha and I drank our first post-pregnancy wine together. In fact, when my husband and I were looking to buy a house, Natasha told us about Whispering Willows, and obviously, the rates here were really high by then. But we just *loved* the apartment—it's one of the few duplex units, you know—and the fact that we'd be so close to Natasha and Vikram made it completely worth it.'

By this point, I was beginning to think that if I asked Smita what her family's annual income was, she would happily tell me.

The sound of the front door opening made both Smita and me turn. Aahan, Smita's eleven-year-old son, came bursting in, calling loudly for his mother before realizing she was right there. In a span of a few seconds, he had skidded towards the dining table, gotten rid of his bag, skidded back to his mother, demanded a snack, removed his shoes, magically acquired a football *and* filled his mother in about some big event that had taken place on the school bus.

Smita, who was beaming with joy the whole time, patiently heard him out while giving instructions to the boy's nanny to give him his milk and cheelas. Just as quickly and noisily as he had entered, Aahan disappeared upstairs, and a few minutes later, the nanny followed him up with a tray of food.

Smita smiled broadly at me and suddenly her gaze shifted to just above me.

'Sana! Come, come!' she said brightly and got up to greet her friend.

Sana Hussain was a slender woman with clear, glowing skin, a sharp bob and a well-put-together but casual vibe about her. She was dressed in black sweatpants and a deep red T-shirt that stopped right at the waistband. She was wearing black thong flip-flops with a discreet Tory Burch logo at the 'V', and her expensive athleisure clothes fit her toned body perfectly.

'Sorry I'm a little late, but I wanted to make sure my daughter got home before I came here', Sana explained as she sat down next to Smita.

'Both our kids go to Orion, although Amina is a bit younger', said Smita. 'Now that we're all here, should we have some green tea?'

Before anyone could respond, Smita had called Gayatri and given her instructions on what tea to get, which cups to use and what snacks to pair with the tea.

'Smita was just telling me about how she and Natasha met,' I said to Sana. 'How long had you known her?'

'Oh my god, it's hard to say—it's been that long! We both moved here within a year of each other, but we'd met on and off at the club before that. Gosh, I would say at least fifteen years? She was unlike anyone else—so warm and helpful to everyone. There's not a single resident who didn't know and love her,' Sana said, her eyes filling up and her voice quivering.

Smita reached out to hold her hand, and they sat quietly for a few seconds. The genuine friendship and sense of loss the two women shared was palpable, and I felt like an intruder in that moment. I looked down at my notebook and scribbled some notes—fifteen years, popular, what club?

Sana was the first to snap out of it. She wiped her tears and smiled at me. 'It didn't matter how long you'd known Natasha for her to make you feel like you were a really special friend. She introduced Smita and me, and the three of us bonded so quickly, all thanks to Natasha.'

'Forget the two of us, I can't even tell you the number of times she's stepped in for other residents. People would call on her to pick up their kids from the bus stop or receive a package for them. It's not as if the others wouldn't do the same, but you just never felt any hesitation about asking Natasha,' piped in Smita.

'I think the only time I've ever seen her not get along with someone was that incident with that little girl's mom— what was her name?' Sana looked at Smita, her brows furrowed as she tried to jog her memory. 'You know, on the WhatsApp group?'

'Oh yeah, but that woman is a cow. She's still on the class group and is apparently still constantly picking fights with everyone. But the fact that she managed to get a rise out of Natasha just tells you how much of a cow she is,' Smita said.

'Really?' laughed Sana. 'But what had happened exactly? Natasha never really got into it with me.'

'You know how kids are. Apparently, one of Natasha's boys had said something rude to a girl in his class, and instead of texting her privately, the girl's mother, Charu something, sent this long, hateful message on the class group. I think Natasha was in her Pilates class, and she didn't see it until much later. But by then, Charu got so mad at being ignored that she practically started yelling at Natasha on the group.'

'Oh my god, that's horrible! Who does that?' Sana exclaimed.

'Oh, I've heard many stories about her. Here, try these quinoa puffs with the green tea. They're so yummy and I think quite healthy only. They're baked, you know.'

———

'You don't do lactose-free milk? That just won't work—I just can't digest lactose. Now if I ask for almond milk instead, you'll charge me extra, and that's not fair, right? You can't penalize someone for food allergies that are beyond their control. Tell me something, are you vegetarian? Imagine if someone charged you extra to not serve you non-vegetarian food? Do you think that is right?'

The lady ahead of me in the coffee shop line was clearly on the warpath, and her victims already included the hapless barista behind the cash counter, the ever-growing line of caffeine-starved customers behind her and all logic of any kind.

I looked at the barista to give him a half-smile of commiseration and then turned sideways towards the table where Jaya was scrolling through her phone. Slim to the point of appearing frail, with a thin face and long, somewhat wavy hair that was often bundled away into a messy bun, Jaya had the kind of beauty that wasn't obvious right from the start. She had large, serious eyes that gave her face an almost stricken look. It was only after a few minutes of conversation that she would suddenly be tickled by something someone had said and break into a smile.

Break out a smile—it's like that phrase was created for Jaya, for her smile was nothing less than the sun breaking out from behind grey clouds. It was so big and warm and unexpected that you couldn't help being dazzled by it, and the transformation it brought to her! In a split second, she'd go from a slightly forlorn and possibly hungry girl to the most stunning creature on earth. The change was remarkable, and its effects stayed with you.

My roommate, Aalia (whom, I just realized, I haven't even mentioned so far—that's a complete travesty—you'll definitely be hearing more about her later), had once made an astute observation while we were watching *Friends* on my laptop, one that could possibly apply to Jaya as well. See, both Aalia and I felt that Courteney Cox's Monica was the prettiest of the three girls, and we couldn't understand why they kept harping on about Jennifer Aniston's Rachel being the one every guy in New York wanted. My weak theory was that perhaps beauty was judged differently in the '90s, but Aalia's was more compelling.

There was a certain type of girl, she said, who was immediately attractive to boys but whom no other woman would ever categorize as such. It was like a secret memo had been circulated only amongst the male of the species. 'She, that regular-looking girl with rather average features? *She* is beautiful. Now go.' And then the boys would universally fall for her in droves!

As Aalia and I explored the idea further, I grew more convinced that she might have a valid theory. Both of us could remember girls in school or college who came with the reputation of being super hot, and both of us remembered being completely underwhelmed and actually rather puzzled when we first laid eyes on them. And yet, boys would keep falling for these girls, solidifying their status as goddesses. Jennifer Aniston in *Friends* was a prime example. Scarlett Johansson was another serial offender whom boys spoke about as some other-worldly beauty but whose appeal only few women got.

I suspected that Jaya, with her waif-like features and big sad eyes, was part of the same hallowed group. In a simple black tee and denim cut-offs, she was dressed as unobtrusively as possible, and yet, I could immediately sense the male interest she attracted—from the coffee shop manager who'd helped us find a table to the laptop-toting young man who asked if he could borrow a chair and spoke only to Jaya the whole time.

'Yes, the name to call is Kavita. That's C-A-V-I-T-A. Please make sure you get it right.' Of course. There was no way Lady

Lactose Intolerant was going to pay extra for almond milk and suffer the injustice of a misspelt name. She stood up for her rights and was particular about spellings. Honestly, I had become a fan.

My order was much simpler, and I cut the poor, harassed barista some slack by asking him not to warm up the food. It was all different forms of sugar and would taste amazing anyway. Soon, with my tray piled up with two coffees, a brownie, a muffin and a cinnamon bun to go (a little something to nosh on for later), I made my way back to Jaya, eager to share highlights from my afternoon and get her inputs.

'Oh my god, Sana is so hot! I mean, not just for her age. She's just all-round classy and so posh,' gushed Jaya. 'I totally want to be her when I grow up. And she's a really good mom, I think—like, very devoted.'

'I think all moms are devoted to their children. Once you've lugged them around in your belly for nine months, I'm guessing they become a pretty important priority,' I said.

'Ah, you'll be surprised, babe. Once you've hung around these ladies for as long as I have, you can tell the good moms from those who should never have been allowed to have kids. I don't know, I feel like once their kids are in school, the mums feel like they've done their bit of child-rearing and it's time to move on to other things. It's like the child-raising takes a back seat, and other things come to the fore.'

That was a pretty extreme thing to say, I thought. And more than a little judgemental. But who was I to disagree with Jaya, a woman on her way to do a prestigious master's programme in education policy, so I just smiled and waited for her to tell me more.

'Okay, so Sana is really into healthy eating and stuff for her daughter. Easier said than done, of course, because the only thing kids apparently want to eat is sugar. But Sana came up with these innovative recipes that are healthy and delicious, and kids love her food. In fact, I know Sana has been trying to become an influencer for some time now. Mommy influencers are a big deal, but as you can imagine, it's a pretty saturated market.

'Natasha, on the other hand, had gained quite a massive following on Instagram without even trying. Like she used to just post stuff about Pilates and art and her kids without an agenda, and poor Sana, who is actually really talented—she even hired a photographer to film her recipe videos—has been struggling to get new followers.'

Jaya lowered her voice. 'But let me tell you what happened just a few weeks ago. Sana had made these amazing gluten-free cookies with, like, honey from emancipated Himalayan bees and conflict-free almond flour and butter from cruelty-free milk. I don't know, it's a whole thing. So anyway, Sana shared the cookies with Smita and Natasha and asked if Natasha would share them on her Instagram, and get this, Natasha said no!'

'What? *Why*? I thought they were best friends?'

'Right! That's what Sana thought too. She was sure Natasha would never turn her down, and she was quite taken aback and hurt. Natasha claimed that her Insta was for herself, not to endorse products, and that she didn't want to get into "that game", Jaya said, miming air quotes. 'But Sana was like, "I'm not asking you to endorse anything. I'm your friend. You said these cookies are delicious. Just write about them. What's the big deal?"'

'And what did Natasha say?'

'Natasha stuck to her guns. And later, she told me that *she* was offended that Sana had put her in such an uncomfortable position. Frankly, in this case, I felt for Sana. She wasn't asking Natasha to do anything unethical or outrageous—just post about cookies that were genuinely delicious and free of, you know, all the things you want them to be free of.'

'That's so strange,' I mused, 'Especially coming from someone like Natasha, who everyone swears will go to the ends of the earth to help you.'

'Hmm ...' said Jaya, looking at me with her eyes slightly scrunched up, like she was trying to decide whether she should speak freely or hold her tongue.

'What?' I asked.

'I'll tell you, but it's strictly off the record, okay?'

'What? No! Okay, tell me and then I'll see.'

'No, no, there's nothing to see. Off the record or I'm not telling. In any case, it has no bearing on your story on her and her Lake Ahilya clean-up drive.'

'Aarrgh! That's not fair,' I mock-shouted.

This really was a weird situation to be in, and all of a sudden, I couldn't decide if Jaya was a source or a friend. Why was I even entertaining these thoughts? Of course she was a source, and this entire conversation and the coffee were to get a more detailed profile of Natasha. But there was no law against befriending a source, was there? We were sort of the same age—Jaya was just a few years older than me— and we genuinely seemed to get along.

Eventually, my curiosity got the better of me, and I swore I wouldn't include her information in my story.

'So Putts's bachelorette trip? Natasha organized the whole thing, including when to go, where to go and exactly which hotel to stay at …' Jaya stopped talking, picked up her muffin and took a dramatic bite, all the while looking straight at me.

I looked back at her dumbly, waiting for her to finish eating and tell me more.

'Don't you get it? Natasha's air ticket and stay were paid for by the resort! But she didn't tell anyone else that and made sure Putts and all her friends had her bachelorette trip there. Natasha was already a player in "the game"—and there was no way she was going to endorse anyone else as an influencer.'

'*What*? Are you sure? How did she pull that off without letting Putts and the gang know? And how do you even know this?'

'Oh, the hotel was really discreet. Since Natasha did all the bookings, she told everyone that the hotel would make individual bills. So everyone thought she paid the same as them. And as to how I know—well, I have my sources.'

'What sources?' I asked disbelievingly.

'Total fluke, ya. An old school friend works at the hotel's PR firm—she saw me in one of Natasha's Insta posts and casually mentioned that the resort wanted to position itself as a safe destination for solo and groups of women travellers and that her firm had approached Natasha with the proposal.'

'Woah! So why didn't Natasha just tell anyone?'

'Beats me!' Jaya shrugged. 'I thought she'd tell me herself, but when she didn't bring it up, neither did I.'

I sat there, baffled by the information I had just been given. This went against everything I'd heard about Natasha.

How could someone as sweet and helpful and generous as everyone said she was pull off such dishonesty? How could she engineer an entire girls' trip around a freebie she was getting and not mention it even once? This was a woman who had practically brought an entire dying lake back to life, and she'd done it on her own time and her own dime. Why would she lie like this to her closest friends?

Jaya sensed my bewilderment, and her voice took on a gentler tone. 'Hey, don't look so upset. I know we've all sort of sold her to you as this perfect human being, but nobody can be that perfect, right? She *was* all those nice things, and this incident was just an anomaly. This shouldn't change how you write the profile. That's why I didn't tell you, but when you brought up Sana and all, it was just too much for me to keep it in.'

A few tables away from us, Cavita with a C was smiling at a group of friends, picking up her almond milk beverage, laptop, charger, phone, earphones and bag to move to a table for one so that the group of friends could sit at her bigger table. For fuck's sake! Was no one who they seemed any more?

I shook my head and smiled at Jaya. 'This certainly adds a new dimension to her squeaky-clean image, which, honestly, makes her more interesting and real. I'm glad you told me, Jaya. And you're right, I suppose she could have been all these things together, right? Sweet *and* caring *and* generous *and* helpful *and* super conniving? Ha! I think we just found the Meghan Markle of Bangalore's mommy world!'

CHAPTER 10

Later that night, after I'd gotten home, thrown aside my bra, gotten into my home shorts and tee, and was cooking a gourmet meal of Maggi and Fanta for Aalia and myself, my conversation with Jaya kept niggling at me. The dirt on Natasha may be off the record, but I knew I could trust Aalia with it. I would swear her to secrecy, and besides, whom would she even tell at her consulting job? According to Aalia, the only thing that perked up any interest with that lot was tips to get noticed by a senior partner or new methods to be assigned to a project abroad. Anything else was a waste of time.

'Should I order ice cream before it's too late?' shouted Aalia from the dining room, or what we called the Great Hall. It was, of course, neither great nor a hall, but rather a tiny hallway that the landlord had stuffed with this massive but surprisingly beautiful eight-seater dining table. If the chairs were pulled out, one had to squeeze around them to get past the table and into our bedrooms. It reminded us of the long dining tables in Hogwarts, and hence, the tiny dining area was forever renamed the Great Hall.

'Okay,' I shouted back, 'but I thought you said you were quitting all processed sugar.'

'Yeah, from tomorrow, na? I want to have my last unhealthy meal of Maggi and ice cream tonight, and I'll be golden tomorrow.'

For all the years I'd known Aalia before we were roommates, she was always quitting some food or the other. (We were expressly forbidden to use the word 'diet' for its connotations of patriarchy and other man-made evils.) So far, she had quit (and then re-embraced) meat, dairy, carbs, breakfast, dinner, breakfast and dinner, bananas, caffeine, all white spirits, all dark spirits, Facebook, Instagram and Snapchat, all in an attempt to lose weight. Strike that—to get fit and be her best self. Her friends and family kept telling her that she already was an excellent version of herself, but she insisted that beneath five kilos, there lay hidden an even more superior version. And she owed it to the world—and to herself—to let Best Aalia out.

For tonight, however, I was just going to have to make do with sub-par Aalia to discuss and dissect the day's proceedings. I told her everything: about my visit to Smita's apartment, complete with detailed descriptions of her house and maid and green tea and delicious baked-not-fried snack, about Sana and how polished she was, and finally, about my coffee with Jaya and all those revelations she had unloaded on me.

'Well, first, you're clearly an amazing journalist who can get her sources to spill anything and everything,' said Aalia. 'So three cheers to that, woman!'

'Well, the part about Natasha being an influencer and getting her holiday for free was off the record, so ...'

'Yeah, that's the part I want to discuss. I promise we'll discuss Natasha properly, but I'm really puzzled about why Jaya told you any of it. If she claims it doesn't affect your story, then why even share it?'

As Aalia was saying it aloud, I knew immediately that what had been niggling at me was not Natasha's duplicitousness but the fact that Jaya told me about it. Yeah, sure, finding Natasha's body had brought us together, and we did get along, but still, we'd only known each other a few days, and our relationship was mostly professional.

But instead of following that line of thought, I found myself defending Jaya 'You know, I think she just needed to get it off her chest. I mean, it's a pretty juicy bit of information to be carrying around with absolutely no one to share it with. And at least she was considerate enough not to sully Natasha's reputation by telling her friends about it. Come to think of it, I kind of get why she told me.'

'Hmm ...' said Aalia as she scraped the last bits of chocolate sauce from the indented base of her plastic bowl.

'What else could it be? She asked me not to write about it, and I won't. She insisted that Natasha really was as nice and genuine as everyone says she was. I think she needed to tell someone and she did, and that's that.'

'Okay.' Although she was clearly not satisfied, Aalia could tell that I was done with the topic and decided to change it. 'Dude, how does one become an influencer with 25,000 followers and get free trips to Thailand, ya? I also want!'

'All right, so here's what I know. You gotta find something that's dying, like a lake, or an art form, or a person, or a democracy, or whatever. Just find it and revive it. And you do it while being nine feet tall with perfect skin and a certification in Pilates. Although, I think, yoga might also do. Then, you post about it constantly on Instagram and spit, spot, there you have it—free trips, baby!'

'All I heard was "post constantly on Instagram". I think you, me and my last ice cream ever deserve to go on the Gram. Pout please,' Aalia instructed as she angled her phone above our heads and captured us with our empty bowls. #ByeByeSugar, #Roomies, #NewBeginnings, #HealthFirst.

———

'Hello? Hi, Sana, I'm well. How are you? No, no, it's not a bad time at all. Tell me. Oh yes, yes, Jaya told me you bake wonderfully. I'd love to try some of your stuff. Oh. You have a stall at a flea market this Saturday? I see. All home chefs and mom entrepreneurs? That sounds interesting. Yeah, I don't know if I can do an exclusive feature on you because our food reporter does that, but I'll check if I can do a write-up on the flea market and mention your stall. Okay, sure, I'll drop in. Yes, around 3 p.m. Trinity Gardens? Yep, done. Okay, see you.'

'Babe, some mommy-led flea market this Saturday. Probably be boring but should have good food options sans processed sugar. Come, na! 🙏*'*

'Hey! I was thinking of going anyway. I'll see you there. What time you planning to go?'

'Also, I'm totes fine with processed sugar! 🍩*'*

Oh fuck! Had I just sent a message meant for Aalia to Jaya?

CHAPTER 11

Sahil was mad at me. Why else would he send me forty kilometres out of the city to cover the interiors of a farmhouse belonging to some unknown architect couple? He also assigned me Moses, only the surliest photographer on our roster of freelancers.

As we drove in silence, I tried to be efficient and get some work done. My interview with Putts was fixed for the next day, as was a call with Babu, who was also going to give me the names of some members of the Clean Ahilya drive. I'd still not contacted Natasha's husband, Vikram Babani. I just wasn't sure how soon was too soon to call a grieving husband and father and ask him questions about his wife. What if he started crying? Would my classic hand-on-the-shoulder manoeuvre work? Would it even be appropriate? I'd have to ask Jaya about it on Saturday now that I'd begged her to come to that dumb flea market with me. I cringed at the memory of that direct message mix-up and wondered if I should tell Aalia or just let the thing pass. If only I had a normal person in the car I could talk to and not Mr Mute Moses, who refused to do anything but glower and take fantastic pictures.

With talking not being an option, I opened my phone and started browsing through the architect couple's Instagram page. It was mostly offices, tech parks and a couple of malls, and while they certainly had a diverse range of projects, there was nothing that I hadn't seen before. From neatly organized open offices and colourful breakout rooms to restaurants done in an industrial style with cement walls and exposed pipes, it all looked quite familiar. At the end of the day, I supposed, even the most creative architects had to cater to their clients' requests. I hoped their farmhouse would be more inspired, though.

Sixty excruciatingly quiet minutes, three BuzzFeed quizzes and one true crime podcast later, we were finally at our destination. As we drove in through the high wooden gates and down the long driveway, my spirits started to rise. This place was freaking gorgeous! For one, the majority of the five acres it was built on was mostly vegetable patches and fruit orchards. It was only towards the end of the road that the couple had built a mid-sized cottage with a little lawn in front. Somehow, they'd managed to make it look rustic and plush at the same time, and this kind of chicanery was *exactly* the sort of thing that impressed me.

Chhaya and Stanley Prabhu, husband and wife and co-founders of Prabhu Design, were already standing outside, ready to greet us with big smiles and glasses of pomegranate juice, which I later discovered were from pomegranates grown in their own orchard. They appeared smart and warm, much like their home, and my irritation with Sahil started to thaw a little. Perhaps this long drive to the outskirts of the city wasn't a total waste of time after all.

Quick introductions were made, the juice was consumed and the Prabhus began a tour of their property. Moses was clicking away in the beautiful, natural afternoon light, while I took copious notes on how they grew only local fruits and vegetables and recycled their water supply, what composting methods they used, and what was behind their decision to keep everything as sustainable as possible. With the outdoors covered, we then moved indoors to check out their beautiful white home built around a courtyard paved with the most striking red sandstone.

Moses took a quick look around and started shortlisting spots to set up his equipment, while I was given a more detailed tour of the house. It was a simple home with a large hall, an open kitchen and dining room, and three bedrooms and bathrooms, but the care that had gone into designing every element was evident. High ceilings and big windows to let in as much light as possible, comfortable furniture to sink into, a long table in the kitchen, perfect for entertaining friends, wall art that was a mixture of upcoming artists and their own children's paintings, a large pantry stuffed with non-perishables, shelves of books and board games—this was a home you could tell they escaped to often.

Across the red courtyard were the bedrooms, and Chhaya Prabhu started by showing me her kids' rooms, when I spotted a bright green sweatshirt folded neatly on the bed with the words 'Clearwood Academy' embroidered into it.

'Clearwood Academy,' I wondered out loud. 'Now why do I feel like I've heard that name before?'

Chhaya looked mildly puzzled. 'Clearwood, that's the school my kids go to. They're in grades six and four.'

'I'm sorry, I'm not originally from Bangalore, so I'm not very familiar with the schools here,' I said, trying to explain my confusion. 'But I feel like someone just mentioned it to me recently.'

'Well, it is one of the most well-known and, dare I say, best schools in Bangalore.' Chhaya smiled. 'Have you seen the loft we have made for the kids here? The high ceilings of the house allowed us the space, and it's quite a handy area for them to tuck away all their books. We put in these high transom windows so they'd have plenty of natural light to read.'

The loft was definitely very cosy and an absolute dream for anyone who loved to read, or waste time on their phone, or just lie down and gaze at their acres of farmland. This house was perfect in every way, and I'd already decided to convince them to rent it out to struggling journalists on weekends.

'It's a child's dream,' I gushed. 'We need to get Moses to come up here and get some aerial shots. He might have to hang by the fan, though, haha!'

'Oh, we have a ladder he can use,' said Chhaya, completely missing my morbid joke. 'Here, let me show you the bathrooms,' she said, leading me through a bright blue door. 'We use solar panels to heat the water, and there is a skylight that keeps it brightly lit till almost five in the afternoon. And the kids really fought with us on this, but we insisted on no showers in any of the loos. It's such a waste of water, and there's nothing more efficient than a bucket bath.'

I popped my head into the bathroom to check out the famed bucket and skylight, and as I looked at the washbasin, I again spotted a Clearwood Academy memento, this time in the form of a green ceramic mug holding two toothbrushes and a tube of toothpaste.

Clearwood … Clearwood … Why couldn't I place where I'd heard this name? And why was this annoying me so much? Had Jaya studied there? I knew Smita's son went to Orion, which was, of course, an IB school and very expensive. 'Oh *yes*—of course!' I suddenly whispered out loud.

'Excuse me?' said Chhaya.

'Sorry, I just remembered where I'd heard the name Clearwood,' I explained. 'I was supposed to interview someone whose sons study there. Unfortunately, she passed away in an accident …'

'Oh, you knew Natasha Babani?

'Sadly, I never got to meet her, but I have heard so much about her,' I said. 'Did you know her?'

'Well, our kids are not in the same class, but the Clearwood community is really tight and we all pretty much know each other. It's a small school, you know—just one section per class until middle school, and there are never more than thirty students per section. Also, her husband and Stanley are both ex-Clearwood, and we often bumped into each other at alumni events. Every time I met her, she was really so warm and friendly. I'm having a hard time believing she's no more—we all are.'

'Damn, I can imagine how shaken up your family must be,' I said sympathetically. 'It is a very shocking thing, what happened.'

'Yes, our family is, but so are all the Clearwood parents and staff. So many from the Clearwood community showed up at her cremation. And many, many more at the prayer meeting afterwards. It was quite a sight to behold. But then, this school is special like that. We're like one big extended family—we watch out for each other.'

'Wow, that's pretty unusual for a school,' I marvelled.

Chhaya smiled. 'Like I said, it's a special place. I sometimes tease Stanley that one of the reasons I married him was because he's a Clearwood alum. I never studied there, but I always knew I wanted my kids to go to Clearwood.'

'Wait, what do you mean? Do only the children of ex-students go to Clearwood?'

'It's not a rule or anything, but yes, kids of Clearwood alumni get first preference, and being a fifty-year-old school, there are quite a few of them! I remember when my Aanya got into grade one—that was six years ago—after giving alumni kids and siblings of existing students admission, they had only two slots left. My god, it was a bloodbath. More than 500 kids had applied; the school administration was practically batting away desperate parents willing to do anything to get their child in.'

500 applicants for a seat in class one? What the hell was this school? 'I don't get it. Why the mad rush for a spot in class one?' I had to ask Chhaya. 'Are the kids guaranteed a spot in Harvard or something? What's so special about this school?'

Chhaya let out a short laugh that was part smugness, part pity for my ignorance. 'It's *Clearwood*, my dear Sneha. Everybody wants to be in Clearwood. It's a fabulous school, featured for decades in all the lists of India's best schools. And to answer your question, yes, several Clearwood kids go to Harvard. And Princeton. And Stanford. It's exactly the kind of foundation you want to give your child.'

Chhaya looked at my gobsmacked expression and shrugged. 'I know it feels like I'm showing off, but I really am proud to be Clearwood mom. However, I think we've gotten derailed with all this talk of schools. I'd love to show you one of the prettiest parts of this farm—our very own ancient banyan tree. It's at least 100 years old, and we wanted the master bedroom to have a door opening right to it. It's gorgeous, and whenever we're here, I always have my morning coffee under it. Come, right this way.'

———

As we drove back to the office, for once, I was glad that Moses had such a strict no-talking policy. My head was spinning with thoughts of local red tiles and ancient banyan trees and bathrooms without showers and schools that were harder to get into than the Prime Minister's office. I couldn't quite reconcile these two facets of Chhaya's personality—her warm, grounded, solar panel–loving side and the side that couldn't stop gloating about her kids' school.

A *school*, for god's sake. A place meant to provide what was the fundamental right of every child. Sure, I know we live in a deeply unequal society where basic amenities, like education and healthcare, varied wildly depending upon your income level. But today's conversation hinted at a divide that went beyond wealth. It spoke to connections and pedigrees and the privileges of old money that no amount of wealth or hard work could buy. I felt like I'd taken a wrong turn and walked into a very exclusive VIP room in what was already an exclusive club. This was a room you couldn't buy your way into. You were either a member or you weren't, and the only people who decided who became a member were already inside the room.

I couldn't imagine what this must do to those on the outside, clamouring to get in.

CHAPTER 12

'Sneha. SNEHA! Sneha, wake up! Wake up! Your phone's been ringing off the hook.'

My phone? Wait, what? What time was it? Had I ordered groceries online and chosen the early morning slot again? Aalia? What was Aalia doing here?

I forced myself to open my eyes and tried to get a grip on what was happening. Aalia was in my room, on my bed, waving my phone in my face.

'What happened? Is everything okay?' I asked groggily.

'It's your phone, babe. You left it in the Great Hall. I don't know how you didn't hear it. It's been ringing non-stop for at least an hour.'

'Shoot, I'm so sorry!' I said, still confused and disoriented. 'What time is it? Am I late for work?'

I looked at my phone. Wait a second. It was 6.52 a.m.—practically the middle of the night. Who the hell calls at 6.52 a.m., and why the hell had they been calling for a whole hour?

I unlocked my phone and saw two missed calls, both from Jaya, one at 6.50 a.m. and one at 6.46 a.m. So my phone had been ringing for six minutes, which Aalia had slightly exaggerated to sixty.

'It's Jaya,' I said, still dazed and even more confused than I had been a moment ago.

'Jaya? What does she want? Maybe she found another body. Call her back!' said Aalia, pushing her glasses up her nose.

'Okay, okay, hang on. Let me just sit up at least.' I really hoped Jaya had not found another body. It was way too early in the morning to deal with such morbid news, and frankly, stumbling across one dead body in a lifetime was quite enough.

'Jaya, hi. Yeah, yeah, no it's okay ... I mean, yes, I was sleeping, but I had to wake up in two hours anyway ... No, no, it's fine ... It'll be nice to see what the world looks like at dusk or dawn or whatever this time is called.'

I widened my eyes and shrugged at Aalia, who was gesturing wildly for me to get on with it. That girl had no patience even when she was well-rested, and she was being positively manic right now.

'Oh, really? Smita told you that? Woah! That is big news. I would've woken you up too. You think it's true—can't be, na? Yes, please find out more and call me any time ... No, no, I'm glad you called. I've been meaning to get up early, so this is great ... Yes, later.'

'What? What is it that she had to call you at the crack of dawn for?' Aalia shouted, having lost all patience.

'Calm down! Jaya was out on her morning walk, and she met Smita, who told her that there's a rumour that the police are going to open Natasha's file again because somebody called and said that her death couldn't have been an accident—she might have been murdered!'

I was obviously foolish to expect such news to have a calming effect on Aalia.

She now stood up and started walking around my room with her hands over her head. 'What. The. Actual. Fuck. Murdered! Oh my god, Sneha. Shit! Who do they suspect? Are you two suspects? Woah!'

'No! Why would we be suspects? I didn't even know the woman. I don't know whom they suspect. Jaya will find out more and keep updating me. But this is unbelievable! Natasha Babani, the most beloved woman in central Bangalore, whose only crime was to have lied about a free holiday, which is a scandal for sure but certainly doesn't warrant murder! Who could possibly wish her any harm?'

'Call Jaya back and find out who she thinks did it,' Aalia said, picking up my phone.

'Arre, she doesn't know anything. It's just a rumour she heard from Smita. Can you please sit down?'

'You're right, I'm too wired. I need some caffeine. I'm going to get a Coke. Do you want one?' Aalia started walking towards the Great Hall.

'First of all, it's seven in the morning, which just does not feel like a decent time for a Coke. Second, you're off processed sugar, remember?' I reminded Aalia as I got out of bed. 'Maybe we should get some tea or coffee or something. Do we have milk in the house?'

Neither of us could remember ever having bought milk, but we did have a vague memory of buying a Nestle Coffee Mate, which we found surprisingly quickly in our kitchen cabinet. Well, not too surprising, I supposed, as the only other things in the cabinet were a packet of dry pasta, a bottle of something called Italian seasoning and a bar of chocolate (sugar-free).

Coffee Mate found, the only thing we now required was coffee, which we did find, albeit as a hard, coagulated mass that had gone from brown to black, with some suspicious flecks of white on the side.

We had no choice. We would have to change, wear sneakers and go somewhere that served coffee by walking out of our home into this early morning world of newspaperwalas, walkers, school-going children and god knows what other freaks who felt the need to be out and about at this time. All this was happening thanks to a woman I'd never even met. I swear to god, Natasha Babani, if you weren't already dead, I'd kill you myself.

One of the most wonderful features of Bangalore are its darshinis, the city's version of fast-food restaurants, in every neighbourhood, which serve fresh vegetarian food, like idli, dosa and vada, juice, chaat and also, inexplicably, Chinese food, paneer butter masala and butter naan. What was even better was our discovery that several of them opened quite early in the morning and sold excellent coffee at Rs 20 a glass.

'Why do we ever go to Starbucks?' Aalia asked, sipping her coffee and trying her best to enjoy it even without the sugar.

'Oh, I don't know. For the chance to say "grande" and pretend that we're fancy global citizens. Shit like that costs money, you know.'

'True, true,' said Aalia, sagely nodding her head. 'Plus, we can also choose a to-go cup and walk around the city like we're in an episode of *Gossip Girl*. Walking around with a little steel tumbler just doesn't feel the same.'

'Another good point, and there's the air conditioning and the free Wi-Fi,' I added.

'Absolutely right. Add them up, and it makes perfect economic sense. And my mother says I don't value money. Little does she know,' snorted Aalia.

'Speaking of money,' I said, 'I was just wondering—if Natasha was murdered, do you think it was for money?'

'Did she have a lot of it?' asked Aalia.

'Well, going by her apartment and lifestyle, she was obviously well-to-do,' I said. 'But I don't know if it was family money or if she was independently wealthy. She used to be a chartered accountant before she had her twins, so she must've been good with saving and investing.'

'Plus, she had all that influencer money,' said Aalia. 'If it's murder, it must've been the husband. It always is. That is, unless, they had a butler—then the police have their work cut out for them.'

I burst out laughing at the thought of a Mr Carson-like character in Natasha's life. Although if any woman was posh enough to lord it over a butler, it would have to have been the late Mrs Babani.

'Let's see. I'm going to meet bride-to-be Putts today. I wonder what she'll have to say about this new angle.'

'Oh yes, I'm sure she'll have a lot of juicy goss. Listen, since we're here, should we get some idli-vada? I'll go order, and you make sure no one takes my seat. Babe! You need to stretch your leg out and put it on my stool so everyone knows it's taken. I can already see many vultures waiting to grab my spot!'

CHAPTER 13

Premanjali Bhat, aka Putts, worked at a fancy financial services company with offices in a fancy business park that also housed several other fancy organizations and fancy eateries. For the second time that day, I found myself holding a table for two at a coffee shop as I waited for Putts to come and join me. In our interactions on WhatsApp, she had sounded extremely polite and extremely busy, but had been nice enough to carve out an hour to speak to me about Natasha.

At the stroke of 11.30 a.m., our appointed time, I saw a striking woman in an understated grey-and-pink linen saree walk in through the glass doors of the coffee shop. Even before I'd gotten up to meet her, her sharp eyes spotted me, and she walked over to my table.

'Sneha?' she asked, putting out her hand to shake mine. 'Hi, I'm Premanjali.'

'Lovely to meet you, Premanjali. Thanks so much for meeting me,' I said as we shook hands and started to sit down. 'Can I get you a coffee or something to eat?'

'I just had something at a meeting a little while ago,' Premanjali said. 'But why don't you go ahead?'

'Oh, I'm good too,' I said. 'Already had quite a bit of coffee today.'

'So tell me, what do you want to know?' said Premanjali, getting straight to the point.

'Well, like I said, I'm doing a profile on Natasha Babani and wanted to interview a few of her close friends. Do you mind if I record this?'

'Not at all, go ahead.'

'So, can you tell me about how long you had been friends?'

'Well,' started Premanjali, 'I'd known her since we were in school. She was actually my younger sister's classmate, and the two of them were very close. I'm six years older than them, and I lost touch with Natasha after I went to college and eventually got married. Then, a year or so ago, my teenage daughter and I moved to Bangalore, and Natasha reached out to me. Moving to a new city and a new job can be overwhelming, and Natasha was nothing less than a guardian angel to us. To be perfectly honest with you, most people don't quite know what to do with a divorced mom who has moved cities to be with her boyfriend, but having Natasha embrace us like she did just erased all the awkwardness we might have experienced.'

Wow, Premanjali was pretty forthright, I thought as I scribbled furiously in my notepad, wondering what to ask her next—more questions about Natasha or how come she had a boyfriend and I didn't.

'That sounds exactly like the Natasha everyone describes,' I said, 'extremely friendly and warm.'

'She was by far the most thoughtful and generous person I'd ever met. You obviously already know how full her life was, with her kids and her Pilates and her friends, and yet, she managed to make space for me and Vaanya—that's my daughter. She was an absolute rock and went out of her way to help us settle down. You know, I once asked her where to buy good prawns from because Vaanya loves prawn curry and, of course, she instantly shared her prawn guy's number— Natasha had a guy for everything. Then two days later, she showed up at our apartment with a box of prawn curry that she had made! She was like that, really thoughtful and giving.'

Premanjali sighed. 'I'm getting married in a few months, and as this is my second marriage, I was keeping it quite low-key. But Natasha would have none of it—she insisted I celebrate it like the special occasion it is and organized a girls' trip for a bunch of us to Thailand. Sadly, that was the last time I saw her ...'

I gulped at the mention of the Thailand trip and muttered some platitudes about life and how uncertain it was. There was no way I could bring up the free airplane ride and hotel stay without breaking my promise to Jaya, and it wasn't important to the story anyway.

'Congratulations on your wedding, Premanjali. When is the big day?' I asked.

'We're planning a small ceremony in December, easiest time for my sister and parents to come down,' she replied.

'If you don't mind my asking, you said people don't know what to do with a divorced mom. What did you mean by that? I mean, haven't things changed from our parents' time? Does it even matter to people your age or if you're divorced or married or unwed or whatever?'

For a second, Premanjali stared at me like she couldn't tell if I was being serious or not, and then she started to laugh. 'Well, Sneha, first, I think your parents and my parents belong to two entirely different generations. But to answer your question, in my experience, when you get divorced, that's how people identify you. In any case, in the workplace, the tags are always "woman manager" or "woman VP" or "working mother". When you get divorced, you're known as "that single mom who has done well for herself".'

'And how do people perceive you in a social setting?' I asked.

'As a total anomaly, of course. By my age, we're all expected to exist in pairs, especially if you're a woman. When I meet other parents at Vaanya's school, almost nobody ever asks me what I do for a living. The first question is always, "What does your husband do?" When they find out there is no husband, well, the conversation gets very, very quiet.'

'But that's ridiculous in this day and age!' I blurted out. 'I know so many women who are single moms by choice. There's a lady in our office who had a baby through a sperm donor, and nobody treats her any differently.'

'Have you ever spoken to her properly about her experience?' asked Premanjali gently.

'Well ... no. But her child is in kindergarten, and she seems really well settled, and her parents support her and everyone in the office loves the kid ...'

Premanjali shrugged. 'I hope it continues like that for her, but I think she might be letting on only part of the story. How do I explain it? Things nowadays are not like the Middle Ages, where the townspeople gathered together to stone us single mothers. It's more subtle. It's in the omitted invitations to social events or in the strange mix of pity and awe people start viewing you with. Can't blame them, really. I think we're so used to things being a certain way that we just don't know how to react when the script changes even a little bit.'

'Wow, that's ... disappointing,' I said.

'Disappointing, frustrating, unfair, saddening—it's all that but it's also just the way it is. But you know what, every once in a while, you get lucky and come across someone like Natasha who doesn't care about any of that and is there for you with all she's got. All because, and I have no recollection of this, you apparently bailed her out when she flunked her Hindi exam in class six by pretending to be her older sister and speaking to her teacher.' Premanjali laughed. 'I don't know how on earth we got away with it, but Natasha swore that's what happened and claimed that that's when she pledged her undying loyalty to me.

Taking a breath, Premanjali continued, 'You know, Sneha, she really was an absolutely exceptional human being. I don't think the enormity of what's happened has fully sunk in for Vaanya and me. She'd become such a big part of our lives in the last year that I just don't know what we're going to do without her.'

Both of us sat quietly for a few seconds; Premanjali seemed to have drifted off into another world, and I was busy absorbing everything she'd said while trying to build a narrative around it. The coffee shop was almost entirely empty, and the girl behind the counter was quietly engrossed in updating some sort of ledger.

The bright, midday sun streaming in was tempered by the film on the windows, and everything around us was unnaturally peaceful and perfect. Suddenly, I was filled with a deep sense of fatigue, like I was out of my depth with this story. What was the point of it again? That Natasha was a nice person whom everyone was going to miss now that she was dead?

Just then, the door to the coffee shop opened and two girls with bright red lanyards dangling around their necks walked in. The girl behind the counter looked up from her ledger and started to prepare herself to smile at her customers. But before the girls with the red lanyards could get to the counter, one of them looked at her phone and let out an angry 'Shit, ya!' Her boss had just pinged her and they would have to go back up to office. Her friend rolled her eyes and made some remark about her needing to learn to push back.

'Yeah, yeah,' the girl with the difficult boss muttered, and although they'd both turned around and I could see only the back of their heads now, I could sense her frustration with both her boss and her lecturing friend.

'Premanjali, I wanted to ask you something,' I said, now that the peace was shattered. 'I found out this morning that the police may be investigating Natasha's death as suspicious. They've been asked to reopen the case. Do you think it's possible that there was foul play involved?'

My question took Premanjali by surprise, which was followed by anger. She frowned and asked me brusquely, 'Who asked the police to reopen the case?'

'I don't have all the details yet. I heard from one of her neighbours.'

'Sounds like a bullshit rumour to me. And I'm really not sure if it's appropriate for you to be asking me this.'

Her sudden aggression threw me for a second until I remembered that I was completely justified in pursuing whatever information I had. 'I'm not going to publish it without verifying it,' I said, sounding more defensive than I wanted to. 'I was simply wondering if you had any thoughts on this line of investigation.'

Premanjali leaned back in her seat and stared at me for a few seconds. I could tell she was trying to size me up while carefully calibrating her response. Eventually, she took a deep breath and said, 'I can't imagine anyone wanting to hurt Natasha.'

'So you think it's impossible that someone caused her death?'

'Look, as far as I am concerned, Natasha only wished everyone well. But I can't vouch for the others in her life. Who knows what drives people? So if you're asking if it's likely if someone killed her, I'd say no, but is it possible? What can I say—anything is possible. You'll just have to follow up with the cops on this.'

***

'She's a total badass type, ya—obviously super bright and highly skilled. They don't just make anyone vice-president. She must run a super-tight ship and 100 per cent signs off her emails with "PB".'

Aalia giggled. 'I need these reports in an hour! Signed, Peanut Butter!'

'Oh yeah!' I laughed. 'Man, I hope she's marrying someone called Jamal or Janardhan or something like that. PB and J are a match made to last.'

'What's she like to look at?' asked Aalia.

'Super attractive in a dusky, tall, ethnic jewellery-wearing kind of way,' I said, trying to think of whom she looked like. 'She was wearing a pretty linen saree with chunky silver jewellery that could be from Amrapali or Tribe and thick eyeliner.'

'What kind of blouse was she wearing?'

'Oi, why is the blouse important? You sound like a pervy stalker!'

'You know I need to form a complete picture in my head of all these people,' Aalia persisted. 'Was it one of those designer, printed blouses that you could never imagine would go with a saree but totally does, or was it one of those matching blouses that one needs to cut from the saree?'

I stared at her and shook my head in disbelief. Aalia was prone to bouts of nonsense, but I think this lack of sugar was messing with her brain more than ever.

'It was a matching pink blouse. My god, Aalia, your love for detail is *ridiculous*.' Giving her a look, I continued, 'And before you ask, it had a deep back and those little cap sleeves only people with skinny arms can wear. I can imagine Jaya wearing a blouse like that and looking great.'

'Ah,' said Aalia.

Suddenly, I felt the energy in the room shift, as though the temperature had dropped several notches. 'What?' I asked.

'What what?' said Aalia.

'Why did you go "Ah" like that?'

'No reason. I was just picturing PB—got a pretty good image,' said Aalia.

'I don't get it. First you have a hundred questions about what she looks like and what her freaking saree blouse is like, and then when I give you all the details, your only response is "Ah"?'

Now Aalia looked genuinely confused. 'Sneha, why are you getting so worked up? What did you want me to say?'

Why *was* I getting so worked up? The drop in warmth I'd felt from Aalia had been real, right? One minute she couldn't get enough information out of me and the next, she'd suddenly gone all silent. Only because I had mentioned ... Jaya. It was her name that had caused this, I was sure of it. Or was I? Suddenly, I didn't know what was real and what I'd imagined.

'Nothing,' I said softly, feeling quite foolish. 'You're right. I just figured you'd also want to know what kind of footwear she was wearing.'

'Well, what kind was it?' asked Aalia.

'I don't know. I never got a look at her feet.'

'I hope it was nice,' added Aalia sportingly. 'I hate it when people ruin a good outfit with bad shoes. God, I hope it wasn't one of those shiny V sandals with wedge heels.'

'Yikes! No, no! I'm sure they were either cute Kolhapuris or some stylish kitten heels—you know, sensible but pretty work shoes.'

'You must go back tomorrow and find out. It's your duty as a journalist to get the complete picture,' Aalia said.

'Ha ha! Sure, I'd definitely go back only to check her shoes, but tomorrow is Saturday, my darling, and you and I are going to that mom entrepreneurs' flea market thingamajig.'

And meeting Jaya, I added in my head. But it didn't feel right to say that part out loud.

———

As I was scrolling aimlessly through my Instagram feed later that night, I saw that Jaya had posted a story about her cycling slowly in her complex. 'Cycling for the first time since the accident. Guess riding a bike really is like a riding a bike.' She'd added a smiley emoji at the end too. I was about to react with the applause emoji but stopped myself. I switched off my phone screen and turned to go to sleep. A minute later, I picked my phone up again, scrolled back to her story and threw in the applause emoji. Jaya would know I'd seen her story anyway, and now I felt compelled to react to it.

Damn you, Instagram, and your lack of privacy features. From now on, I was going to stick to stalking people quietly on Twitter and Facebook.

CHAPTER 14

'Welcome to the Village Bazaar, ladies. Thank you so much for encouraging our mom entrepreneurs,' said the incredibly handsome young man at the welcome desk of the flea market.

'You're most welcome,' gushed Aalia. 'We love moms. I have a mom. And so does she!'

Oh, Aalia.

'Haha, that's good to know,' laughed Handsome. 'I was raised by wolves myself, so I'm trying to get my quota of maternal love by hanging around these amazing ladies now.'

'Oh, so you're what Mowgli grew up to be,' shot back Aalia, not ready to throw in the towel after her 'I have a mom' PJ.

Handsome was hooked and stuck his hand out. 'You got me. My cover is blown, though. I go by Samar now. Nice to meet you …'

'Aalia, and it's nice to meet you too, Samar slash Mowgli.' Aalia shook his hand, charm oozing out of every pore of her body. 'This is Sneha. She's here to make your moms famous.'

For the love of god, Aalia, please stop!

'Is that right, Sneha?' Samar turned his attention to me, bestowing on me another gorgeous, although less flirty, smile.

'Hey, Samar! I'm with Cactus. I was in touch with Bhavna from your team. I told her we'd be doing a small write-up of the event for our website.'

Samar seemed entirely clueless about our visit and started rifling through a diary on his table for any evidence of my conversation with Bhavna. 'You know, Bhavna seems to have forgotten to update the media list, but that's fine. You guys go on ahead and I'll connect with her later. Here, let me put these wristbands on for you first.'

Aalia stuck her arm out and purred, 'Well, look at you handing out free wristbands like it's no big deal.'

'Mowgli has some special perks like that,' said Samar smoothly. 'Sneha, here's a free one for you too.'

'Gee, thanks,' I said, rolling my eyes, partly impressed, partly embarrassed by Aalia's smooth flirting.

My eye roll and attempted sarcasm were completely missed by Samar, though, who was still grinning at Aalia as he wrapped the bright pink paper band around my wrist.

'Do you mind if I take down your contact details, though?' asked Samar, opening his useless diary once again. 'I'll need those to follow up on the story.'

As I scribbled my number and email address, Aalia fiddled with her wristband, while Samar turned to attend to another group standing behind us. After all that cheesy back-and-forth, I couldn't believe they stopped short of exchanging numbers.

'Have fun, ladies!' Samar cheerily waved us in. 'And don't forget, we're doing this for the moms.'

'What happened back there?'

'I don't know, you know.' Aalia shrugged, obviously less affected by this failed attempt to mate than I was. 'He either chickened out and didn't ask for my number or just lost interest. Super cute, though.'

'He was hella cute, and the way you two were going on, I thought I'd have to leave you there with him and go into this mom fest all alone.'

Aalia put her arm through mine and squeezed it affectionately. 'My darling Sneha, you've helped me yank out the world's most stubborn chin hair when I'd all but given up on it. I could never ditch you, no matter how cute Mr Mama's Boy is.'

'Oh yes, that was quite an operation, wasn't it? Although, you know, Vij was saying you should never pull out chin hair. She said if you pull one out, you incur the wrath of all the other surrounding hair follicles, and they start sprouting like mad in an act of revenge.'

Aalia looked at me, completely terrified. '*What*?'

'Apparently, when she was in her twenties, she pulled one out, and by her mid-thirties, she could pass for a sixteen-year-old boy who hadn't started shaving yet. But I think she's had laser or something done, and it seems to be under control now.'

'The actual fuck?' gasped Aalia, rubbing her chin worriedly. 'So what are we supposed to do when we see a chin hair now? Just let it keep growing and then shampoo and condition it?'

'According to Vij, cutting is better than plucking. Don't worry, when we get home, we'll look online for a good deal on men's trimmers and shavers for you,' I said soothingly.

Aalia laughed and pushed my arm playfully. 'Just you wait,' she said. 'I'm going to grow out that damn thing, and you'll have to stare at it all day long.'

'Yeah, yeah, I've seen worse. Okay, chalo, now let's go see what these mom entrepreneurs have been up to,' I said. 'Let's start that way, from stall number one.'

The Village Bazaar had been designed like a cosy little seaside hamlet, the kind most likely to be seen in a Hallmark film. All the stalls were blue and white and sported little flags with the stall number and the name of the particular business. Fake lamp posts with baskets of fake flowers were placed at equal distances from each other. Boards with titles like 'Ye Olde Cloakroom' and 'Ye Olde Tavern' directed you to the loo and food stalls. There was even a town crier who was making announcements about special promotions and offers over the PA system, starting with 'Hear ye, hear ye!' The whole thing was terribly pretentious, but at the same time terribly enjoyable.

What was a revelation, however, were the wares these cute stalls had on display. I'd expected the same old mix of jewellery and blankets sourced from Rajasthan along with the usual array of brownies and healthy oatmeal cookies. But the ladies at this market had outdone themselves. Stylish lamps and lampshades, gorgeous home linen and unusual pottery, children's furniture, jams and pickles made of fruits I'd never heard of before, tons (and I mean tons) of ready-to-eat and ready-to-cook food made from millets—the stuff these moms were peddling was hardcore.

There was an all-ladies outfit that set up waste-to-compost machines for all sizes of home, ranging from bungalows to apartment complexes. There was a collection of STEM (science, technology, engineering, maths) toys designed by moms who clearly knew their target audiences well. And most importantly, this was a village unsullied by pesticides or chemicals of any kind, and everything was organic or personalized—or both.

I found myself admiring an adorable little blue checked dress for a three-year-old that the stall minder informed me was made from a fabric called Vichy that she had sourced from France. She claimed that Kate Middleton dressed her kids in the same fabric, and it was the best you could give your kids. I told her I'd make a note for when I had kids and politely asked the price so that I could include it in my story.

'My clients are mostly international,' she said, 'and our pricing is in dollars.'

'I see, I see,' I said.

'This one is from our Daily Tumbles collection and retails at $150. But I'm giving a 10 per cent discount to all our Village Bazaar customers.'

'Right, right,' I said as my brain went into overdrive with some quick mental math. *That can't be right,* I thought, even as I deducted 10 per cent from the total. Had she actually priced a dress for a toddler at over Rs 10,000? Was this legal? I slowly backed away from the stall, scared to sneeze or even breathe near this most precious item of clothing.

Nearby, a stall called Touch Wood was selling DIY wooden kits for kids to assemble and paint. I picked up a basic 6X4-inch picture frame and balked at the price tag— Rs 2,500 for four pieces of wood, a mounting board and a piece of glass! Were there no pricing guidelines applied to anything on sale here?

Wow, I thought, suddenly starting to see all these businesses in a new light. When it came to kids, your basic food, clothing, shelter, education and television were clearly not enough. You could sell these parents anything, and they'd pay obscene sums of money for it. Had I made a mistake in becoming a journalist? I mean, I knew there was no money to be made in the profession, but nobody told me the alternative was selling crayons in the shape of the letters of the alphabet.

In my exploration of the Village Bazaar, followed by my existential crisis, I'd managed to lose Aalia and suddenly spotted her approaching me with a little paper bag in her hand, looking mighty pleased with herself.

'Ta-da!' she announced triumphantly, holding the bag up like a trophy. 'I've decided to start cooking at home and have just bought my first appliance.'

This was what happened when they paid you so well at these consulting companies. I groaned inwardly, shuddering at the thought of whatever overpriced piece of junk Aalia had just picked up.

'What is it? I asked tentatively, 'And why is it so tiny?'

'Stainless steel sandwich cutters in the shape of a star and a butterfly, guaranteed to make the fussiest eater gobble up whatever sandwich you put in front of them,' declared Aalia with a big grin.

'Oh my god, Aalia! What healthy sandwiches are you planning to make?'

'Chill, ya,' she laughed. 'They're for didi's kids. She's been trying to switch them to ragi bread, and they're having none of it. So I thought these might help. I don't know why she can't stick to the normal maida bread like God intended us to eat. I can't wait for this healthy eating fad to go away. It's totally outlived its natural lifecycle!'

'Says the girl who has given up processed sugar,' I pointed out.

'You know I'm a slave to these trends. Speaking of which, where are the healthy desserts you promised me?'

'Sana said she was in stall forty-nine in the food area,' I said, checking my phone. 'Follow me.'

Sana Hussain's food stall, simply called Sana's Desserts, was one of the prettiest stalls in Ye Olde Tavern. She had a whole pink, blue and white, floral, English afternoon tea theme going on, complete with cloches, multi-tiered cake stands and little cups with saucers. Amongst the pies and cupcakes stood Sana herself, understated and classy as ever, in a light blue shirt tucked into the world's best-fitting jeans, with diamond earrings sparkling through her immaculate bob.

As soon as she saw me, a warm smile spread across her face, and she waved me over to her stall. 'Good to see you, Sneha,' said Sana. 'Thank you so much for coming.'

'Not at all,' I said. 'We're having such a great time! This is a very well-organized event.'

Turning to my roommate, I made introductions, explained Aalia's food restrictions and congratulated myself on bringing her to the right stall. Turned out, Sana was also dead against processed sugar, and all her desserts used alternatives like honey, dates, maple syrup or coconut sugar. Aalia and I quickly ordered and paid for a slice of cheesecake and banoffee pie each and sat down to enjoy our desserts while Sana dealt with a big group that had just descended on her stall. As was the norm in this place, each dish was outrageously priced, but I would be reimbursed by my office, so it didn't hurt as much.

'Bloody hell, this cheesecake is amazing,' sighed Aalia, licking her spoon. 'I'm going to get another slice to take home.'

'Umm ... my banoffee is fabulous too,' I agreed. 'But at these prices, they'd better be nothing short of life-changing.'

'Yeah,' said Aalia, lowering her voice. 'The prices are a bit much, right? I didn't want to say anything because I thought she was your friend ...'

'Please! I hardly know her—I've met her once before,' I assured Aalia. 'I don't know, babe—maybe these ingredients are like super expensive, or her mark-ups are unreasonable.'

'It's probably a bit of both,' agreed Aalia. 'Ditching sugar is not a cheap commitment, I tell you. I'll just have to stick to Diet Coke for my sugar rush.'

We were wiping our plates clean, making sure we didn't leave a single crumb, when Sana came and joined us.

'I hope you enjoyed the banoffee pie and the cheesecake,' she said.

Her voice was so gentle and polished that I wanted her to give me speech lessons.

'Very much, thank you,' I replied, unconsciously mimicking her soft style of speaking.

'How about a couple of cappuccinos to wash 'em down? On the house,' she said.

Aalia and I began to weakly protest, but Sana was already walking back to her stall and giving her assistant instructions for three cappuccinos, sugar on the side.

'She's so posh!' Aalia whispered to me.

'I know. Now *shh*!' I whispered back as Sana came back to join us at the table.

'So, what do you cover for your website? Because last time you were doing a story on Natasha ...' Sana asked pleasantly.

I explained that I was on the lifestyle beat and covered several city events and happenings. I also explained that I was originally meant to interview Natasha before she died so tragically and that's how I ended up working on a posthumous profile.

'How's that coming along?' asked Sana, handing us the cappuccinos that her assistant had brought, each with a cute pattern in the foam.

'A little slow, actually. I'm yet to interview a couple of people, and now ...' I hesitated, not sure whether to continue.

Sana widened her eyes just a little and she looked at me inquiringly.

'Well, they're apparently reopening the investigation into her death because they think it might not be accidental,' I continued. 'I called the police station today to find out, but they were really tight-lipped about it, neither confirming nor denying anything.'

I laughed nervously. 'I never thought I would ever say that sentence out loud in real life. But yeah, I need to keep that angle in mind as I continue working on the article.'

Sana had clearly known about the reopening of the investigation and didn't pretend to look surprised. She turned around, as if to check on her stall, and then looked at me. 'It's bullshit,' she said. 'Nobody would ever want to hurt Natasha, and she most certainly didn't do it to herself. I don't know why they're dragging this thing on and making it worse for Vikram and the boys.'

'The husband,' I quietly mouthed to Aalia, who nodded impatiently. She was better acquainted with all the characters in Natasha's universe than I was and was probably mildly affronted that I'd felt the need to fill in the gaps for her.

'Well, who could've called the police then?' I asked. 'Could it be her parents? Maybe they're not satisfied with the investigation.'

'No, I think it's someone being malicious. Someone who didn't like her, I suppose. Not enough to harm her or anything but someone who just doesn't want this whole scandal to die. Like some sick person who wants to extend the misery her death has brought.'

'Like who?'

'Look, I have no proof, and I'm not going to name any names. But when you're as popular as Natasha was, you also invite a lot of negativity. I think this is being done by someone who was jealous of Natasha when she was alive and is getting some cheap thrills out of torturing her friends and family now.'

'That's ... that's mean and cruel and just awful! My god, who would do such a thing?' blurted out Aalia. She'd been quiet so far but couldn't contain her shock any more.

Sana shrugged. 'But people are often unkind and petty— and clannish and competitive and, like I said, very jealous. Who knows where these emotions can drive them?'

Sana was being purposely mysterious, and I was getting a bit annoyed by the whole thing. Either name names or don't say anything. This middle path she was toeing was completely unnecessary. But since she wasn't going to say anything, I decided to drop it, ask for one of her menus and get the hell out of there.

Aalia, my ever curious and slightly tactless friend, however, was picking up no such signals. 'But I don't get it,' she said, her voice high, her brows knitted together in a deep frown. 'Who would want to bad-mouth Natasha and torment her family like this? Like other Pilates instructors or Instagrammers or who? And why? This makes no sense!'

Sana stared at Aalia. Her face was expressionless, but her dilemma was plain to see. What should she do? Dish it out to these two obviously inexperienced and slightly silly young girls or maintain a dignified silence?

Finally, she tore her eyes away from Aalia, looked at her coffee and then looked at me. 'You know,' said Sana. 'I worked for many years in advertising and marketing, and after a break, when my daughter was born, I worked with an art gallery. A couple of years ago, I started baking commercially. As you can imagine, each one of these fields can be extremely stressful and competitive. But do you know which one is the most competitive? The one that can take over your life if you lose sight of why you are doing it in the first place and get sucked into this imaginary contest to be "the best"?' She raised her hands to mime air quotes for 'the best'.

'Advertising?' I said tentatively, knowing fully well it was the wrong answer.

'It's motherhood,' said Sana softly. 'I know, I know, motherhood is supposed to be this great, selfless, unconditional thing we do, with no goal other than to raise happy, healthy children. But somewhere along the way, it's become the most competitive race in the world, with the goalposts constantly changing, and it's bloody hard to keep up.

'Also, and I know this sounds a little harsh, but I think when your main occupation is being a mother and homemaker, when that's all you do night and day, you're more prone to making it a competitive sport. And with competition comes rivalry, resentment and just all sorts of not-good behaviour.'

Mothers? *That* was the big reveal? That it was some other mom who was behind this investigation being reopened? And for no other reason than to ... exactly what?

Sana could tell by our expressions that Aalia and I weren't completely buying her theory, vague as it was, which was good because she felt compelled to explain further.

'Natasha was my best friend, and I miss her every day. She was warm and generous and had the biggest heart you could imagine. But nobody's perfect, right? Natasha had a competitive streak, and she had to be the best at everything. Sometimes that rubbed people the wrong way.'

I was starting to get Sana's point but needed more clarity, and so I pressed on. 'Yeah, but what do you mean rubbed people the wrong way? I mean it's not like there are gangs of moms and she belonged to one and was stepping on someone else's turf.'

Sana laughed. 'Actually, that's a pretty accurate way of describing it. I mean, I've never thought of it like that myself, but you know, there are actual groups of moms and, boy, they can be as vicious as any street gang.'

'*Really*?' said Aalia. 'So which group do you belong to?'

'Oh, the only groups I belong to are my Art of Living group and the Home Bakers of Bangalore group. Those guys know where to get the best ingredients. I have a life outside of being a parent, you know?' said Sana with a tiny smirk. 'It's the full-time moms who're the ones you need to watch out for. In fact, here comes a group now, and I need to go wait on them. I'll see you girls later.'

Sana picked up the coffee cups and gracefully sashayed over to her stall to greet a group of four women and an indeterminate number of kids. All four women were dressed remarkably similarly, in knee-length cotton dresses and sandals embellished with sequins and diamantes. They all wore big sunglasses and had stylish bags slung sideways or on their shoulders.

Going by the chorus of 'Hiiiii!' and 'Good to see you, babes!', it was apparent that they all knew Sana from before. As I observed the meet-and-greet from afar, I suddenly noticed that all the kids had disappeared. I looked around and found them being ushered to some tables near us by a couple of women who appeared to be their nannies. One was helping the smaller kids onto the chairs while the other was handing out wet wipes to the lot.

'Didi, water chahiye,' I heard one of them squeak and saw Nanny 2 whip out a blue-and-silver water bottle from a big Harrods tote she was carrying.

'Sne, things are going to get noisy here. Should we go see the rest of the bazaar?' asked Aalia.

'Yeah, let's go,' I replied slowly, strangely transfixed by the efficiency of the nannies. The tote she was carrying was no less than Mary Poppins's carpet bag and it appeared to be holding more than this entire flea market had to offer. In the few minutes they had been here, she had pulled out wet wipes, water bottles, an iPad, a little dabba of cut watermelon, a packet of biscuits and a juice box. And while all this food and drink was being disbursed, the mothers of these kids were busy ordering up a storm at Sana's and her neighbouring food stalls.

I could've stood there and watched Nanny 2 and her magic Harrods bag for hours, had it not been for an Instagram notification on my phone. It was Jaya, my accidental plus one to the flea market. She had just come in and was waiting for me by stall seventy-eight, Not Just Succulents.

I looked at Aalia and a felt a twinge of … something. This was so weird. Why was I feeling so anxious about introducing Aalia, my roommate and one of my closest friends, to Jaya? Aalia and I were constantly meeting people from each other's lives. We'd studied different courses in college and had several groups of friends that sometimes overlapped and sometimes didn't. Aalia had moved to Bangalore and started work six months before me, and by the time I moved in with her, she already had three different groups of friends who she claimed catered to three distinct moods: office goss, old-town nostalgia and Zumba girls. Through college and now, she'd had one serious boyfriend and dated a couple of boys casually, while I'd had two nearly serious and a number of casual relationships. None of that had ever made things awkward between us. This was ridiculous, I told myself. *Stop imagining things and be normal.*

'Jaya's here,' I said, my voice casual and light. 'She's by some stall called Not Just Succulents. Ugh! It sounds like a sex shop that sells more than just blowjob toys.'

'Oh god, Sneha,' said Aalia, scowling. 'Only you can distort a perfectly innocent horticultural name like that. Although, what would those toys even be like?'

'Hmm … like plungers and suction pumps? Or maybe a fake mouth with a little mechanical tongue?'

Aalia howled with laughter. 'But made with only organic materials because, after all, this is the Village Bazaar.'

'Oh yes, yes! Organic, vegan and completely cruelty-free.'

'And never tested on animals.'

'Euuww! Stop right there!' I cried. 'This way. I think stall seventy-eight is at the end there.'

Standing in front of a perfectly innocent plant shop with no hint of sex toys was Jaya. She was wearing black cotton trousers and a pink cotton sleeveless top with a tiny grey heart embroidered on the back. A simple tan crossbody bag, strappy tan sandals and big silver jhumkas completed what I was gathering was a classic Jaya look.

As if sensing us coming towards her, Jaya turned around and gave me a little wave. 'Hey!' she said as she walked forward.

'Hey, Jaya!' I said, perhaps a little overenthusiastically, suddenly not sure if I ought to hug her or not. Fortunately, she was less awkward and leaned in for a quick embrace.

'This is Aalia,' I said, introducing the two. 'Aalia, meet Jaya.'

Aalia and Jaya greeted each other, and then, for what seemed like an eternity, the three of us stood and stared stupidly at each other. My mind was a complete blank, and for the life of me, I couldn't think of a single thing to say.

Aalia finally broke the silence. 'Jaya, I've heard so much about you. It's lovely to finally meet you.'

Jaya's smile remained intact, but her eyes belied just the slightest confusion. 'Nice to meet you too, Aalia,' she said. 'And how do you two know each other?'

As a person prone to saying the wrong thing at the wrong time *all the time*, I was no stranger to mortifying situations. But never before had I so fervently wished for a passing meteoroid to fall on me and kill me immediately. Any fate would have been preferable to this hell.

'Jaya!' I exclaimed. 'I've told you about Aalia. She's my roommate, and we've been best friends for, like, six years.'

Jaya looked genuinely bewildered because the truth was that I'd never mentioned Aalia to her. How Aalia looked, I had no idea, because I didn't dare look at her. As for me, I probably looked like the flag of China as my face was absolutely burning up with embarrassment and self-loathing.

'I'm sorry, it must've slipped my mind,' said Jaya. 'You guys are roommates—that's so awesome. You must constantly be cracking each other up. Sneha is hilarious!'

'No, no, Aalia is the funny one,' I said, still studiously avoiding looking at her face. 'But you're right, we are always cracking up around each other. We just made this very funny joke about plants and oral sex. It was in the play-on-words category of jokes, but I'll tell you about it later. Did you want to look around? There're several sections we're yet to check out. Ye Olde Apothecary, Ye Olde Crystal Ball Reader, lots of Ye Oldes …'

'I've been seeing people walk around with charcoal sketches of themselves,' Aalia finally said, interrupting my babbling. 'Apparently, there's a really good artist near the balloon-wallah. Should we go there?'

I finally looked at Aalia, gratitude, contrition and love for her big, generous heart flooding every cell. 'Yes, that's a good idea,' I said. 'Thanks, Aalia.'

The three of us headed to Ye Olde Atelier (fuck, this place was *so* pretentious) in silence. I was both desperate for and also dreading a moment alone with Aalia. I knew I needed to clear this weird misunderstanding, but what would I even say? 'Err, Aalia, this new friend I've made, whom I text with constantly and whom I've described to you in ridiculous detail—I just sort of forgot to mention to her in our one million conversations that I live with a roommate'?

But come to think of it, was that really such a crime? It just hadn't come up—my god, why did Aalia have to be so sensitive? Not everybody was like her, you know. Not everybody needed to know what kind of blouse a person had worn to get a complete picture of them in their heads. You know what? This wasn't my fault. And far from feeling bad, I was now starting to get a little mad at Aalia. I *did not* appreciate being held hostage by *her* high standards for *my* behaviour. And after all these years of being friends, if she was going to let a small thing like this get in the way, then well, I really didn't know how strong our friendship was to begin with.

By the time we reached the starving young artist who was so broke that he couldn't afford a haircut, I was very nearly stewing at Aalia. Jaya suggested Aalia get her portrait done first—it was her idea, after all, and it also made sense to go in alphabetical order—and I was glad for some space from her. So, while she sat on a little stool in front of the artist, Jaya and I sat on a bench nearby and I decided to grill her on some Natasha-related news.

Unfortunately, she had nothing new to offer on the police investigation. Smita had told Jaya that the cops had called Natasha's husband, but she didn't know how their discussion had gone. With that line of questioning having gone dry, I decided to shift focus to Sana's revelations from earlier that day.

I told Jaya about our meeting with Sana and her suspicions about some other mom who was behind this whole reinvestigation mischief. I told her how I found the whole theory completely far-fetched and outlandish, especially the whole mommy group/gang conjecture.

'These are grown women, for crying out loud,' I said. 'I'm pretty sure they have better things to do with their time and their brains.'

'Actually,' said Jaya, dragging out the 'aaaa' of the word as she usually did when she was going to make a point, 'Sana is not wrong. I've been thinking the same thing, and I didn't want to say anything because it sounds so bitchy, but, Sneha, I have seen these women up close for nearly a year! It's like a bloody American high school movie, except those usually end with some kind of humiliation at the prom. This nonsense goes on forever! Also, I can't see what the final prize is, but these moms certainly can, and they're not going to stop until they get it.'

'What do you mean "the final prize"?'

'Well, you know what Sana said about the moms making it a competition? That's totally accurate, but it's not just the stay-at-home moms who're competing. All of them are in it, all these different groups with their parenting philosophies and their views on bloody everything—from what to serve at a birthday party to which school to send their precious progeny to. The end goal seems to be to prove not just that their parenting is right and the best but also what others are doing is wrong. It's kind of horrific.'

I looked at Jaya dubiously, not sure whether to believe her but intensely fascinated by her theory.

'Okay, let me give you an example,' said Jaya. 'Natasha was highly involved with her kids' school because, of course, she was Natasha!

'So, I met her one day for something lake-related, and she was really distracted and kept checking her phone, which she was usually very good at not doing. Turned out there was a major brouhaha happening in her Clearwood parents' WhatsApp group. One bunch of parents, headed by a lady called Charu, I think, had approved brown rice for the school lunch menu, and Natasha and her gang were dead against it because their kids were only used to regular white rice. This exploded into a major war between the "Eat healthy and local" group versus the "Don't push your values down my kids' throats" group. It got really messy, and they had to call an emergency meeting to sort this out.'

'What did they do in the end?'

'Oh, Natasha and her team won. They withdrew the brown rice and brought back good old polished white rice.'

Jaya continued, her eyes shining, her mouth curved in one of her smile-smirks. 'You should've seen her that day, Sneha. She was absolutely ecstatic because this fight had been a long time coming. This same group of moms had messed with her just a few months earlier when they didn't let their kids eat the cake at Natasha's boys' birthday party. Seriously, there is no greater event in a parent's life than their child's birthday party, and there is no greater insult than rejecting the food. I think Natasha had been waiting for months to get back at them, and this was her moment of vindication.'

'Why didn't they let their kids eat the cake? Isn't that the only reason to go to a birthday party?' I asked.

'These kids were vegan, and the cake wasn't,' replied Jaya.

'Vegan kids! *What*? Are kids even aware of these lifestyle concepts? I can barely keep track of what's allowed and what's not. How can you expect kids to know? How old are they anyway?'

'Natasha's boys are eleven, and, babe, they know more than you and I put together. All that mindful parenting is making them pretty bright.'

I thought back to my childhood parties of sandwiches, bread pakoras and home-made cake—and that one super-special party I'd had at McDonald's before it became uncool. At the time, though, I was the envy of every other child in my class, and the McDonald's goody bag that all the guests had taken home had been the talk of the class for weeks.

Shaking myself out of my thoughts, I asked, 'But tell me something—how can one possibly cater to all these dietary restrictions at a birthday party?'

'I think you either ask each child what their preference is or you do what Sana does. She makes four types of cupcakes along with the primary birthday cake so that the kids can eat whatever they want. I think she does gluten-free, dairy-free, nut-free and the last is just a cardboard cut-out of a cupcake. Haha!'

Taking a breath, Jaya continued, 'Natasha once told me about a birthday party her kids went to that had a sugar cane juice stall because the parents didn't approve of packaged juices. It was very cutely done and all , but none of the kids wanted sugar cane juice because they had no idea what the fuck it was, and the parents were googling the calorie count in a glass and stepping as far away from it as possible. It was a total flop, but it photographed well, so it redeemed itself there at least.'

'Hey! I'm done,' Aalia's voice called out. 'Who's next?'

Based on our established protocol of going in alphabetical order, it was Jaya's turn next, which meant I would have to sit with Aalia on the bench, a prospect that filled me with anxiety. Fortunately, Aalia had other plans for her time at the bazaar and announced that she was going to use the restroom and look around for a bit while we got our portraits done.

As soon as Aalia got up to leave, I started to feel bad about not wanting to sit with her. What the hell was going on inside my head today? I was yo-yoing between emotions more wildly than normal and was, frankly, getting a little sick of myself. *PMS*, I thought, grateful that we had this wonderful little phenomenon to blame everything, from bad decision-making to weight gain. In the spirit of premenstrual mixed feelings, I offered to hold on to Aalia's portrait while she walked around, which she gladly agreed to.

Jaya was asked to sit on the stool and stay mostly still. This limited the conversation, and so, I stayed on the bench and looked at Aalia's portrait.

The street artist was no prodigy and would've surely starved to an early death in ye olden times. He'd managed to capture Aalia's big eyes, diminutive nose and silky hair with the shaggy bangs. He'd even taken pains to perfectly reproduce the silver Tibetan knot pendant she wore around her neck. But what he'd totally missed was the set of her mouth when she'd utter her devastatingly funny lines, her face deadpan. Or the utter seriousness in her eyes when she'd grill you on trivial details like the type of curls Vijaya, my editor, had—were they small, tight and crunchy or were they big, soft waves—or the exact colour of brown/mustard pants Sahil, my subeditor, wore to work one day. One shade here or there would make the difference between crap and cool, she insisted, and she was right. (And in case you're wondering, his trousers were total crap.)

I wondered what he would do with Jaya, plain at first, shockingly beautiful later. Or how he would've painted Natasha—physically gorgeous in every way, with an exterior that concealed a complicated mind and soul. Or what in god's name he would do with me, constantly sliding up and down a spectrum of emotions and beliefs? I gave out a short laugh as I thought of the confused lady emoji with her hands up in the air, her eyebrows in a high arch. I may as well get a print-out of her and spare this poor man the time and effort.

CHAPTER 15

That night, Aalia and I had our first big fight. Strike that—that night, we had our first-ever fight. In the six years we'd known each other, we'd never disagreed on anything more than a choice of restaurant or what movie to watch—and those never lasted more than a few minutes. Neither of us was prone to sulking or holding a grudge, especially with each other. Those emotions we reserved for boyfriends and our moms. When it came to Aalia and me, it was always us versus whomever. Perhaps that's why we weren't prepared when this argument came along. And neither of us fought fair.

After the flea market, we'd ridden home in silence. It was after we got home that I said something like, 'Are we going to discuss this or what?'

Aalia had sulkily replied, 'What's to discuss?'

That's when the volley of accusations, counter-accusations, teary-eyed defences, sarcastic one-liners and things we would come to regret sooner or later began. I accused Aalia of being jealous of my friendship with Jaya; she accused me of thinking way too much of myself. I insisted that she'd been weird every time I'd mentioned Jaya; she insisted that it was all in my head. I brought up conversations, the things she'd said and the looks she'd given me. She looked at me like I was off in the head. And that's when things took a bizarre turn, and at some point, the term 'gaslighting' was used by both of us to describe the other's behaviour. We started bringing up incidents from college and beyond that had nothing to do with any of this whatsoever. Statements starting with 'I can't believe you'd ...' or 'After so many years of friendship ...' were accompanied by tear-stained faces and sad shakes of the head.

Around midnight, we were both starving and took a break for some instant noodles and Coke Zero. We sat silently opposite each other at our big-ass dining table and felt pathetic about our horrible fight and our crappy food. We'd once tried to get our cleaning lady to cook for us, and while she was happy to get the extra work, Aalia and I gave up after one attempt at vegetable and masala shopping. Besides, both of us ate a subsidized breakfast and lunch at work, and dinner was usually a mix of cheap takeout food, sandwiches and instant noodles.

Tonight, though, the Top Ramen was just not cutting it, and I craved a plate of steaming hot rice (white, not brown) and some simple yellow dal.

Aalia finished her dinner and went to the kitchen. I heard her run the water in the sink to wash her bowl and fork. After a pause of a couple of seconds, I heard her pick up the saucepan the noodles had been cooked in and wash that as well. Then she came out and stood at the kitchen door and looked at me sadly.

'It's true that I was a little hurt when I realized you hadn't even mentioned me to Jaya,' Aalia said. 'I don't know why, but it just felt really awful.'

Sighing, she continued, 'But there's something else. Jaya is not a nice person. She's super judgy and a horrible gossip. She's been bitching to you non-stop about a woman she claims was her close friend, who's now dead, for god's sake. And listening to her today going on about kids, birthday parties and moms was so uncomfortable. But the strangest part is that you don't seem to mind. You're, like, hypnotized by her or something—you just keep lapping up everything she says. What's that about?'

I had one lone noodle left in my bowl, and I decided the best response at the moment was to put all my effort into capturing that single icy cold thread of maida, and so I twisted and turned my fork until finally I just cut the damn thing into pieces and scooped it into my mouth. Listening to Aalia make these pronouncements on Jaya had been difficult, but even through my haze of anger and fatigue, I could see there was some truth in her observations.

What stung like a ton of bees, however, was what she'd said about me. It was mean and below the belt, and pushed me down a spiral of hurt and red-hot anger I'd not experienced before.

'I'm not lapping anything up, Aalia,' I said coldly. 'And before casting aspersions on others, why don't you turn the spotlight on yourself? What gives you the right to stand there and judge Jaya or me? At least we're not attacking and hurting others with our words—which is more than I can say for you.'

CHAPTER 16

When I'd told my mom that I was moving in with Aalia after I got an offer from Cactus, she'd been thrilled for us. My parents loved Aalia and took comfort in knowing that we'd be together in a new city. She did, however, warn me to be careful not to upset our friendship. 'Best friends living together can be great fun, but it can also end the relationship if you don't draw boundaries,' she'd said. 'Remember to give each other space—you guys don't always have to do everything together.'

At the time, her advice seemed hazy and nebulous, and I had dismissed it with a vague nod of understanding. Aalia and I had a wonderful equation, and I was utterly secure in our ability to get past any misunderstanding. That following Sunday morning, however, as I sat in bed, munching on a packet of Kurkure for breakfast, I was completely out of ideas about what to do next.

To begin with, I was feeling too many feelings. I was offended, angry and sad—with a little shame thrown in for good measure. I was also hungry and had considered ordering in a nice English breakfast for myself, but the thought of getting something so extravagant all alone just didn't feel right. Fortunately, I found a packet of Kurkure in my office bag and decided the best recourse was to watch anime shows and eat junk.

Per tradition, I was watching my show on my laptop while simultaneously checking my phone—god forbid I miss someone's Saturday night party pictures or the accompanying life-affirming caption. That's when I came across the hashtag #GoodbyeNatasha.

An impromptu memorial of sorts seemed to be taking place that very afternoon at the Whispering Willows clubhouse gardens, and everyone who'd known and loved Natasha was welcome. Several people had shared the same jpeg with an image of footsteps in the sand and the headline 'Gone, but never forgotten'. The details of place and time were right below.

As I scrolled through Instagram, a direct message notification popped up on my screen. Jaya had attached the same image with the message, 'Thought you might be interested.'

Excellent. I now had plans for Sunday.

(Also, note to self: please get a life.)

———

After sleeping and consuming online content all day—a hilarious new headstand challenge meant to raise money for a serious disease (or awareness for a rare disease, I've forgotten which) had gone viral—I finally stepped out of my room at around 3 p.m. and looked around for Aalia with trepidation. The last thing I needed was her negative energy as I left to meet Jaya. The flat was quiet. Aalia's bedroom door was wide open and the room appeared empty. The absence of her black Mary Jane platforms from near the front door confirmed it—Aalia wasn't home. *Phew*, I thought, *at least I can walk out of here in peace. Also, hmm, I wonder where she's gone to.*

Thirty minutes later, I was at the Whispering Willows main gate. The security guards had been informed of the memorial event, and the usual multistep process was now just one step. I walked in with three other people, all dressed in long kurtas and jeans, who seemed like they were heading to the same event. I myself had no idea what the appropriate outfit for a memorial was and had decided to go with black jeggings and a black T-shirt with the slogan 'There is no Planet B' emblazoned on the back. I'm sure Natasha would've approved.

The lawns outside the clubhouse were full of people of all ages, and they all seemed to know each other really well. As I edged closer, I saw a makeshift stage near the entrance. A standee with a giant vinyl of Natasha's beautiful, beaming face was placed right in the centre. On one side of the standee was a small podium with a wireless microphone and on the other was a table with an open visitors' book. A couple of women, including Smita Dandekar, were buzzing around the stage, and I assumed they were part of the organizing committee.

There were four rows of white folding chairs in front of the stage, and barring three empty spots, they were all occupied by mostly older attendees and a few parents with little kids. Everybody else was either seated on the grass or standing at the back and on the sides. I looked around for Jaya and spotted her near the front, deep in conversation with a middle-aged guy. She looked comfortable and at home here, which was literally true. But the comfort and sense of belonging she exuded went beyond just her residence—she was part of this community, part of Natasha's inner world, and she probably knew most of the people gathered on this lawn intimately. I was starting to feel like an intruder and regretting my decision to come.

I started to slink sideways to as unobtrusive a spot as I could. What if someone asked who I was or how I knew Natasha? Was it normal for a journalist to be so interested in her subject or was it just borderline creepy? I was starting to panic and decided the best thing to do would be to turn right around and get out of there.

I'd barely turned around and taken a few steps when I found myself face-to-face with someone who looked awfully familiar—a tall, slim lady in a purple kurta and green dupatta, her hair tucked in a claw clip and a pair of sunglasses perched on her head. She wore thick eyeliner and her ears were adorned with silver earrings with little elephants dangling on the ends.

We both stared at each for a couple of seconds until the penny finally dropped.

'Premanjali!' I cried.

'Hi! How are you?' Premanjali replied tentatively, still at stage two of the recognition process, aka 'This person looks very familiar but from where, I don't know'.

'I'm Sneha from Cactus,' I said helpfully. 'I interviewed you about Natasha ...'

'Yes, yes, of course! Sorry, it took me a second to place you. Your hair is different, and well, I guess I wasn't expecting to see you here,' she said.

'Yeah, I thought this seemed like a good opportunity to see all of Natasha's friends and family in one place. But I'm also wondering if I should perhaps not be here.'

'You know, I think it's good you decided to come. You'll get a real feel for just how loved she was. Just don't be asking people about their theories of how she died.'

I'm starting to see why you got divorced.

'You can sit with us,' she said.

That's when I noticed she was not alone. Accompanying her was a girl, about fourteen years old, who was obviously her daughter, Vaanya. She looked remarkably like her mother, although not quite as tall and with a plumper, rounder face.

Premanjali introduced us—I said a quick 'Hey' and Vaanya responded with a mumble—and the three of us walked towards the lawn. We chose a shady spot under a tree, possibly a willow, and settled down for the memorial. Premanjali immediately started scanning the place for familiar faces, and I saw her wave and raise a friendly eyebrow a couple of times. Meanwhile, I pulled my phone out to appear busy. I opened Google to check what a willow tree looked like, and the image search promptly confirmed that this was not a willow we were sitting under.

I deleted some old promotional text messages and was just opening Instagram, when I felt a sudden change in the energy around us. I looked up from my phone to realize that the place had gone completely silent. It was like someone had pressed the mute button on the din of people chattering and chairs being adjusted, and all I could hear was a really loud bird somewhere in the distance. I craned my neck to see what was happening and that's when I saw them—Natasha's husband and her two sons had just walked onto the lawns.

The two boys walked in front, with their father right behind them, his hands on both their shoulders.

Vikram Babani looked tired and deflated, but he had a smile on his face that he seemed to be holding on to for dear life. His boys appeared shy and a little overwhelmed. I couldn't tell if they were identical twins or if they just looked alike the way most eleven-year-old boys looked alike—tanned and skinny, with hair that matched their effervescent little pre-teen spirits. They were both wearing loose jeans and T-shirts—one green with a white robot on it, the other a grey-and-white baseball T-shirt with raglan sleeves.

As they approached the stage with Natasha's picture on it, someone in the crowd started to clap, and very quickly, the others joined in as well. People began to stand up, and in seconds, the whole place was on its feet and applauding, with a few cries of 'Woo-hoo!' and 'All right, Natasha!' thrown in for good measure. I stood up and clapped softly, touched by the atmosphere and also mildly embarrassed for some reason. Next to me, Premanjali was cheering and clapping with her hands above her head, tears streaming freely down her face. Her daughter had been holding her mother's kurta all this time, and Premanjali enveloped her in a side hug.

With everyone standing, I had only a partial view of Vikram and the boys. He too seemed to have hugged his sons and could be seen smiling and nodding at the crowd. The cheering and applauding showed no signs of abating, and finally, Smita decided to take things in her hands and stepped onto the stage and picked up the mic.

'Vikram, Aarav and Siddharth, we're so grateful you could join us today as we remember our most favourite person in the world, our wonderful and amazing Natasha.'

Massive applause from the crowd.

'Guys, we've kept seats for you, so please sit down. We only have this space for two hours, and I *know* our late president would not want us exceeding our allotted time, so let's get this memorial started!'

More woo-hoos.

'We're here to remember and celebrate a person none of us will ever forget. A person who has touched so many of us in so many ways and whose absence we all feel every single day. We want to give as many of you as possible a chance to come up and share your memories and stories of Natasha, and to be able to do that, we'll need some ground rules.'

I had to admit, Smita outside of her marble monstrosity of a house was a much cooler Smita. She was relaxed, articulate and doing a great job of managing the event. She rattled off some rules about where to form a line and how long each person could speak, and even included a joke about keeping the language PG-13. She then called on Mrs Pais's junior choir to begin with a song dedicated to Natasha.

The next few hours felt like an open-air show, like one of those concert in the park events in New York that you only see recordings of on YouTube. People came and shared deeply personal and heartfelt stories about Natasha and what she had meant to them. Kids came on stage and thanked Natasha Aunty for all those times she got them muffins and cold coffee after swimming class. Older neighbours recalled that time Natasha had helped them accept the delivery of and assemble a dining table or made an emergency run to the pharmacy. It seemed like every other resident of Whispering Willows kept a spare key at Natasha's house and had reached out to her multiple times over the years to check for a leak or water their plants while they were on vacation.

Because this was Whispering Willows and everything was done in style, a snack table had miraculously appeared on one end of the lawns midway through the memorial. Vaanya was going over to get her mother a cup of coffee, and I decided to accompany her out of sheer nothing-else-to-do.

As we stood in line for our refreshments, Vaanya plugged in her earphones and started fiddling with a Spotify playlist on her phone. The girl was clearly going through a no-talking phase, and I had nothing but respect for her decision. I may have been well into my twenties, but I distinctly remembered being a teenager, and nothing was more annoying than being expected to chat with a stranger your mum had shoved upon you.

'Babe, I'll tell you. I signed him up for IHeartMath two months ago, and I can't tell you how much it's helped! He goes twice a week, the teacher is old school and his basics have gotten so strong that it's totally been worth all the kicking and screaming I had to put up with in the beginning.'

I turned around to see two women with coffee mugs and biscuits deep in conversation on a bench nearby. One looked very worried, and the other seemed intent on placating her fears.

'Yes, but my husband will be so mad. He's like, "Why are we spending so much on their school if we have to send them to tuitions?"'

'See, that's just it. It's not tuitions—it's just a way to get them to revise and strengthen important concepts, babe. And abhi, they're in grade one. Once their foundation is strong, they won't need any extra help. In the future, they'll be able to keep up with whatever they're taught in class.'

Worried Mom looked entirely unconvinced.

'Okay, how about this?' said her enthusiastic friend. 'Don't think of it as tuitions. Think of it as an extracurricular class. Danesh is going for football and guitar anyway, right? Think of it as another evening activity where they have fun solving maths problems.'

Worried Mom burst out laughing. 'That will probably work with my husband, but Danesh will not buy it for a minute!'

'What to do, ya? Things are so competitive these days, and if these things can give them a bit of an edge, what's the harm, I say.'

Vaanya and I had finally reached the refreshments stall and I got myself a coffee and two pieces of biscotti (not biscuits, as misreported earlier). I could only hear snatches of the conversation now, and it seemed to revolve around maths teachers, current and past. I thought back to my own school and my relationship with maths, a subject I'd always loved. I'd had the most wonderful teacher in classes seven and eight, and the first thing she'd done had been to remove all fear of maths from each and every one of us in class. From there on, numbers became my friends, and I loved the thrill I got from balancing an equation or proving a theorem. I wondered if class one was too young to start panicking about your child's maths foundation, but then, what did I know?

Up on the makeshift stage, after tactfully trying to get a friend of Natasha's to wrap up her reminiscing, Smita had finally jumped up and taken the mic from her hand. 'Guys, we could all be here for another two hours, and we'd still have more to say about Natasha. But we are running out of time and I'd like to invite one last very special speaker, after which we'll have another musical performance to end the memorial.'

Smita turned her gaze towards the front row, tilted her head indulgently and said in a dramatically low voice, 'Vikram ...'

As the man walked on stage, a hush fell over the lawns and everybody stopped talking, sipping, munching or doing whatever they were doing to listen to the grieving widower.

Tall and big, with very fair skin and a light green five o'clock shadow, Vikram Babani cut a sympathetic figure as he fumbled adorably with the mic.

'Hi, everyone,' he said, his voice deep and soft. 'Being here today and listening to everyone has been ... just incredible. What Natasha meant to me and to the boys, we cannot express in words. Without her, it's like life has lost all colour, and as you can imagine, we've been feeling very sorry for ourselves lately. But listening to all of you today gave me a new perspective. I was so busy being sad that I hadn't taken time to acknowledge just how lucky I was to have actually been married to Natasha for fifteen years and to have known her for over twenty. She was and continues to be an inspiration on how to live with love and selflessness. If she achieved so much and touched so many lives in her few years on earth, imagine what she could've done had she not ...'

Vikram's voice cracked, and he paused. Then he smiled and brought the mic closer to his mouth. 'From the bottom of my heart, I want to thank each and every one of you here today who came on stage or spoke to me privately. I especially want to thank Natasha's friends who organized this memorial. You don't know how healing this has been—Aarav, Siddharth and I will forever be grateful.

'Oh, I'd also like to say—while we've really been enjoying all the delicacies you've all been sending over, I'll have to request you to please stop. Mary, whom some of you may know as our cook but who is currently our life support system, is starting to feel a little offended now,' he joked. 'Thanks once again—this has really meant a lot to us.'

With that, Vikram jumped off the stage amidst loud applause and cheers. The super-efficient Smita was somehow simultaneously leading him back to his chair and getting Mrs Pais's junior choir up on stage, where they quickly took formation and started belting out 'Candle in the Wind'. With the sun setting and the kids singing, the lawns now took on a complete concert-like atmosphere. People were singing and swaying, and I even saw a lighter or two lit up, only to be quickly extinguished by the organizing committee. Whispering Willows had strict rules about lighters.

Suddenly, it hit me that the particular moment was either the best or worst time for me to introduce myself to Vikram and ask him for an interview. Before my mind went into a spiral debating myself, I decided to just take the plunge and got up and walked quickly towards him.

Vikram was sitting like an uncomfortable chief guest at a local school function—his gaze fixed determinedly on the stage but his thoughts clearly somewhere else. His sons were balancing a phone discreetly between them, trying to watch or play something without making it too obvious. Smita was in a huddle with her fellow organizers, and before she could intercept me, I took a deep breath and walked right up to Vikram.

'Hi, Vikram,' I said, squatting next to his chair. 'I'm Sneha Talwar from Cactus. I don't know if Natasha had ever mentioned it, but I was supposed to do a profile on her and her work on Lake Ahilya. In fact, I'm the one who found her that day, in the lake, along with Jaya. I was wondering if I could speak to you—not right now, of course—but later, whenever it's convenient.'

The right way to accost a stranger, I've now learnt, is to say hello, allow them to register your presence and then dole out information in small, digestible bits. But the way I'd approached this was what you would categorize as the worst fucking way.

Vikram looked at me with a mixture of surprise and confusion that quickly turned into irritation. 'I'm sorry, what? Who are you?' he asked.

'Sneha Talwar. I was doing a profile on Natasha for our website, Cactus. I was supposed to interview her the day she had her accident.'

'Okay. And what do you want to do now?'

'I'm sorry, I should explain properly,' I said, almost toppling over in my uncomfortable squatting position but somehow managing to hold on valiantly. 'My website was doing a profile on Natasha for her work on the Clean Ahilya drive. While I didn't have the opportunity to interview her, I've gotten to know a lot about her through her friends, and she seemed like a remarkable person. With some help from Jaya, Smita and Sana, I'm doing a posthumous profile on her for the website, and I was hoping I could speak to you as well.'

'You're doing a profile on my wife?' asked Vikram, still confused but significantly less irritated.

'Yes, I've been speaking to her friends and her Clean Ahilya team members, and I would really like to get your inputs as well. If you have an hour or so this week, I could come and meet you and ask you a few questions.'

Mrs Pais's junior choir had finished singing by now, and from the corner of my eye, I could see Smita sweetly helping the children off the stage. And I could also see that from the corner of her eye, she had spotted me talking to Vikram. That was enough for her to go from sweet matron to drill sergeant, and in seconds, the last startled child was brusquely shoved off the stage and Smita was standing next to me and Vikram.

'Sneha! I didn't know you were going to be here,' she said a little too loudly.

'Hi, Smita,' I said, uncomfortably standing up. 'Jaya asked me to come and I'm so glad I did. This was just amazing and so wonderfully organized.'

'Thank you,' she said coolly, too shrewd to be softened by my weak attempts at flattery. 'I wish you'd told me you were coming. I would've organized a seat for you in the front.'

'Oh, it was pretty last minute, and I didn't know you were in charge. I sat with Premanjali and got a good view of everything. It worked out just fine.'

'You know Premanjali?' Vikram asked, standing up.

'I interviewed her for the profile,' I explained. 'And well, I'd really like to interview you as well.'

'Oh, Sneha, I don't think this is the time or place—' Smita started but was interrupted by Vikram.

'Sure. I'd love to talk to you about Natasha,' he said. 'Can you send me an email about this? And I'll get back to you with a good time and place.'

As I took down Vikram's email address, I did an internal somersault of triumph. I felt like a true-blue journalist—I'd spotted an opportunity, accomplished what I'd set out to do (sure, I could've just as well gotten his number from Jaya and texted him, but this was cooler) *and* managed to stick it to these self-righteous ladies who seemed to think they knew better than everyone else.

I thanked Vikram and Smita and walked off to find Jaya, feeling far more confident and at home here than I had two hours ago.

An hour later, Jaya and I were ordering beers and masala papad at a cheap and cheerful little terrace bar nearby. Jaya, who had never been there before, was utterly charmed by the place, and I promised I'd show her other gems like it around the city. It was only fair—Jaya had introduced me to the rarefied world of Whispering Willows. I was going to return the favour by showing her how to live and party cheap in Bangalore.

Besides, with no best friend in my life any longer, what else was I going to do?

CHAPTER 17

Monday morning, 10 a.m., my desk.

I was drinking sugary office coffee and checking how many steps I'd done so far (411) when a WhatsApp notification from an unknown number popped up on my screen. I opened it to find a one-word message: '*Hey*'.

That was it. No introduction, no reason for messaging, not even a punctuation mark—just a lone hey.

I tapped the sender's display picture—a rock perched on a cliff, clearly a stock photo—to see who dared bother me on a slightly hungover Monday morning with their poor WhatsApp etiquette.

Samar B
~Nothing to see here~
11 July 2019

It was the hunky guy from the reception counter at the flea market. What was he doing messaging me so early in the morning? Had he finally worked up the courage to ask me for Aalia's contact details two whole days after they'd met?

I stared at the screen and turned the phone over. No way was I responding to his unqualified 'hey'. If the guy needed something, he'd better ask for it quickly.

I put the phone in my pocket and walked to the pantry. If I was going to hit 10,000 steps, I needed to make sure every step was counted. As I walked back to my desk, my phone beeped again. Samar B again.

'Hey! Just wanted to check when the write-up on the village Bazar will be on ur website. Can u send me the link when it's up. TQ'

He'd misspelt bazaar, used incorrect punctuation and still hadn't identified himself. It was lucky he was good-looking and personable because he had obviously decided to coast through life on those two traits.

I texted back, *'Sure, should be up in a couple of hours. Will send the link.'*

Samar responded with the folded hands emoji, which was lazy but better than the thumbs up emoji, which I loathed. Aalia and I had discovered our mutual hatred of the thumbs up two years ago. We agreed that at best it was patronizing and lazy, and at worst it was a coward's way of saying 'fuck you' without actually saying it. Responding to a text with a thumbs up was like saying, 'I've read your message, and its shit. You're shit. I don't know what else to say, but I really want to end this chat so please stop and let's not talk again.' Aalia and I swore never to use it with each other, and even at our busiest, we'd send each other a simple 'KK' but never ever a thumbs up. We'd planned to one day start a petition to have the emoji removed from the set altogether, but like several of our other grand projects, we had never gotten around to it. The way things stood now, who knew if we ever would.

I felt a sharp pang as I thought about Aalia, about how we'd not spoken to each other since our big fight on Saturday night and how we'd gone to great lengths to avoid each other. She had already been in her room by the time I got back from drinking with Jaya last night, and she had left for work early this morning. I wondered for a minute if I'd overreacted to what Aalia had said about Jaya and then remembered how sweet Jaya had been last night.

We'd gone up to her apartment after the memorial, freshened up and then gone to The Distillery, where we'd ordered several pitchers of beers and had the best time making fun of everyone else at the bar. Jaya's sense of humour was sharp and biting, and her eye-roll game was top-class. She told me she hadn't dated since her accident because she was focused on getting better and heading off to the George Washington University in a couple of months. Although she'd got a fair amount of financial aid, she'd still needed to borrow money from her parents for the course, and she intended to get a job in the US once she was done studying and pay them back. There would be plenty of guys to date there, and she didn't want any romantic entanglements coming in the way of her plans.

Jaya was only three years older than me, but she had her life figured out far more than I could ever imagine doing. She was the kind of person who actually had a detailed, well-thought answer to the question 'Where do you see yourself in five years?' Listening to her gave me mild anxiety, and I felt very small in my low-paying but fun journalism job.

My parents had paid for my postgraduate degree in mass communication, and I hadn't even considered paying them back. Granted, a few lakhs was not really comparable to tens of thousands of dollars, but at this point, I couldn't pay them back even if I wanted to. My salary just about covered my rent, my commute and a sensible lifestyle, and by the end of each month, I was almost always desperately waiting for my next pay cheque. When Jaya made some mention of not wanting to touch her savings, I had taken a big gulp of my beer. All employees of Cactus had zero-balance bank accounts, and I'd taken the zero balance part quite literally.

Suddenly, my phone beeped. Good god, it was Samar B *again* with another lone 'Hey'! What did this guy want and why couldn't he get there already? I waited several minutes for him to follow up the hey with something and when he didn't, I responded with '*What's up?*'

'*This is awkward, but I was wondering if I cud get ur friend Aalia's Instagram handle*'.

And there it was—the *real* reason he had texted me about an article whose whereabouts could be determined with a simple Google search.

'*Let me check with her,*' I wrote back, then turned my screen off, put it on silent and shoved it into my drawer.

Ugh! What to do now? There was *no way* I could send him Aalia's handle without asking her first, and there was *no way* I was getting into a back-and-forth with Aalia about him. As if I didn't have other things to do on a Monday morning than worry about Aalia's potential love life.

I decided not to worry about it for some time and spent the next two hours working on a new trend of Instagrammable restaurants in Bangalore, restaurants where every table and every corner were designed to photograph fabulously. Guests could change their backdrops and play with fun lighting, and the restaurant even provided props that could be used in the photographs.

Moses, the surly photographer, and I had visited two of these last week, and I had to admit, the pictures from my mobile phone camera were almost as good, or at least as exciting, as Moses's professional output. The food tended to be average, with one restaurant perhaps serving slightly tastier food than the others, but that wasn't even the point, so who cared.

The story done, a visit to the loo and 150 steps later, I came back to my desk to see a new email notification on my laptop. Vikram Babani was free to meet later that evening and asked if I could come over to his house.

Why, yes, I could.

⁓

Barely twenty-four hours after my last visit, I was at Whispering Willows again, standing outside the Babani residence. The housing complex no longer intimidated me like it used to—I guess you get used to a place after visiting it 240 million times. But standing outside Natasha's door with the brass lion's head knocker and the shiny plants sent a shiver down my spine. My last visit here had been followed by the discovery of a dead body, and while I wasn't given to superstition, the memory of that day made me uneasy.

Nothing to do but take a deep breath and just ring the bell, I supposed.

Seconds later, I was being escorted in by Vikram Babani. He was dressed more formally than he had been on the day of Natasha's memorial, but his body language and general countenance were far more relaxed.

'Thanks for coming on such short notice, Sneha. I just dropped the boys off at an unscheduled music class, so I thought we could use this time for your interview,' Vikram said.

'No problem. This time suited me perfectly,' I replied. 'Wow! Your home is gorgeous.'

'Thank you. It's all Natasha.'

It *was* all Natasha. Easy, breezy, beautiful without trying too hard, with a few pieces thrown in that surprised and dazzled you. The furniture was mostly classic and white, which could not have been easy to maintain with two kids in the house. It was the accent pieces that created the magic, though. The cushions, the quirky curios, the fabulous artwork on the wall—from paintings and photographs to children's drawings and framed postcards—and the lamps, oh, the lamps!

The Babani home didn't seem to have any visible overhead lights, and after seeing the moody pools of lights created by the lamps all over the house, I immediately vowed to buy a nice lamp for my own room. As it was, our landlord had fitted every room of our house with heavy-duty tube lights, and while they did create a wonderful interrogation room-like ambience, they were less conducive to regular living and even less to romantic encounters of any kind.

'Shall we sit at the dining table?' asked Vikram. 'Easier for you to take notes and stuff?'

The dining table was a more comfortable spot for an interview, and it also had a partial view of the kitchen, where young Mary was busy cooking up a storm. I suspected

Vikram wanted me to feel safe knowing that there was another woman in the house, a gesture I appreciated.

'Right,' I began. 'While writing this profile on Natasha, I've gotten to know a lot about her, and I can honestly say I've never come across anyone like her.'

Vikram smiled. 'No disagreement there.'

'I thought it would be nice to include a little bit about her as a partner and a parent as well.'

'A partner and a parent, huh?' Vikram asked. 'In our time, we would just call it wife and mother.'

'Yeah ... well,' I stuttered, 'I guess we use more gender-neutral language now ...'

'Relax!' Vikram's face broke out into a big smile. 'I'm just pulling your leg. Natasha was a wife and a mother, or, like you said, a partner and a parent, but she was also much, much more. When I first met her, she was working at an accounting firm, and if she hadn't quit when she had, by now she would be regional director at the very least.'

'Mm-hmm ... and when and how did you meet her?'

If I'd had any doubts that Natasha's life was always meant to be a romantic comedy and not a realistic art-house film, Vikram's account of their meet-cute demolished all of them. Natasha Babani nee Sharma, and Vikram Babani had met on an airplane. That's right, folks, the romance gods had decided to listen to the prayers of every starry-eyed girl and horny boy on the planet and decided to make them come true for Natasha and Vikram.

She was travelling to Jaipur for a company offsite, and he was headed there for a cousin's wedding. She'd had to take a later flight than her colleagues for personal reasons, and he had opted for the last flight out so that he could finish working. They weren't originally sitting next to each other, but another passenger requested Natasha to give him her aisle seat because he needed to walk constantly due to his deep-vein thrombosis. Natasha, being Natasha, agreed and ended up next to Vikram.

Vikram and Natasha chatted throughout the flight. Turned out, they had some common friends, and before disembarking, they'd exchanged mobile numbers and he'd texted her his email address so that they could stay in touch. This was the year 2000, and instant messaging wasn't as ubiquitous as it is now. You used SMS for urgent messages and reserved the long chats for phone calls, emails and late-night Yahoo! Messenger sessions.

'So, you got in touch with her after both of you returned to Bangalore?' I asked.

'Actually, no,' said Vikram. 'We were both in line for taxis to our respective hotels, and it was late. And just as she was getting into her cab, I asked if I could drop her to her hotel first and then take the same taxi to my hotel. Told her it would be safer, but really, I just wanted to hang with her a little bit longer.'

I was there in a professional capacity and needed to appear as such, but it took more willpower than I possessed to stop myself from letting out a quiet 'Aww'.

Oh, Natasha, what a charmed life you'd led! If your death had seemed sad and tragic earlier, it seemed positively unfair now. You of the sun-kissed skin, the accountant's brain, the enviable home, the five million friends and the best romance origin story *ever*, you did not deserve to drown at the age of forty-four in a partially clean city lake. You were meant to grow into a handsome old woman and die peacefully in a rocking chair in the veranda of your mountain home, wearing a white pashmina shawl and holding your husband's gnarly old hand. How had things gone so terribly off-script?

'... so yeah, a few years later, we were married, and eleven years ago, we had Aarav and Siddharth,' Vikram was saying.

'Oh, okay,' I said, snapping back to Vikram's narration. 'Is that when Natasha left her corporate job?'

'Oh no, she continued working for a few years even after the boys were born. We had good domestic help, and Natasha was super organized. I thought she was balancing it all quite brilliantly—her office, the kids, the house, our entire lives.'

'Any particular reason she quit?'

'Well, I never really fully understood it, but I guess it's different for men and women, right? It came down to the guilt she carried about being a working mom, which she should not have had because she was always amazing with the boys, very committed and hands-on.'

Were women *still* feeling guilty about being working mothers? I thought that problem had been fixed in the last century with supportive men and that village we'd heard so much about. Wasn't the next thing on the agenda climate change so that we could actually have a planet to pass on to these kids we were so passionate about?

My own mother had worked all her life and was still with the telecom company she'd been at for eight years. Both her sisters were in education, and I couldn't imagine a world where they weren't sitting around the dining table at my grandmom's house discussing colourful colleagues and unreasonable bosses, entitled customers and frustrating students.

I looked at Vikram and wondered out loud, 'Raising twins couldn't have been easy.'

'It's quite a ride,' Vikram said, laughing. 'Those first few months were brutal. And, of course, it's a million times harder on mothers, with all that pressure to breastfeed and the never-ending advice she got from anyone who happened to be passing by. But we got through it, and Natasha was back at work in eight months.'

Vikram paused and then continued, 'From their food to their bedtime routine, Natasha seemed to know instinctively what to do. And she did it all while excelling at her job, until one day, when they were around four years old and in Montessori, she just announced that she was quitting. She said the kids needed her to be around full-time and that was that.

'Initially, Natasha was grateful for the extra time being a stay-at-home mom gave her. She wanted to do something for herself and decided to get back to exercising. She started Pilates at a studio close by and was so good at it that she ended up becoming a certified instructor, eventually conducting classes in the Whispering Willows' gym. She started painting again, a hobby she hadn't pursued since college. But mostly, she spent all her time on our kids—from homework and after-school activities to bedtime reading and those never-ending play dates. Natasha's calendar was always full. And no matter what else she had going on, she always made sure she was at their Montessori school in time to pick them up.

'Once the boys started grade one at Clearwood and were taking the bus, Natasha had more time for herself. She increased the frequency of her Pilates classes and started meeting her friends more often, but she was still as dedicated to the boys. It was only in the last year, after she got busy with the Clean Ahilya drive, that she would sometimes miss a pick-up and send Mary instead.'

'Was she a strict mother?' I asked Vikram.

'Natasha? No way. I've always been the disciplinarian in the family. When it came to the boys, Natasha was just a ball of love. My god, she had endless patience with them. When they really tested her, she would just store all her frustration and take it out on me later,' Vikram laughed.

Just then, the bell rang, and Vikram excused himself to open the door. In the mirror hanging across from me, I saw it was his boys, back from music class. Vikram was smiling, softly asking them something, and the boys were mostly responding in grunts and half-nods. I was struck by the stark contrast between the subdued fashion in which Siddharth and Aarav had entered versus the boisterous entry Smita's son, Aahan, had made when he got back from school. Just a couple of weeks ago, the twins too would've entered their home noisily, happy and secure in the knowledge of a loving mother waiting for them. To see the boys and their father like this, confused and adrift without their anchor, was too much for me, and I felt like I had to leave immediately.

It was one thing to write a story about an unknown woman who had led a seemingly glamorous life and might have a few juicy skeletons in her closet, but it was quite another to be in her home and see the devastation and utter sadness that her death had wreaked. This was out of the scope of my story, and frankly, I didn't have the emotional tools to deal with it.

As the boys headed past the living room and into the bedroom, Vikram introduced me. We greeted each other with muted hellos, and as the boys went off to their room, I told Vikram we needed to wrap up as I had to leave.

'I really only have one more question for you,' I said. 'And it's a sensitive one, but it wouldn't be right for me not to ask.'

'What is it?' he asked warily.

'Are you satisfied with the way the police have investigated Natasha's death?'

Vikram let out a short breath, as if relieved at the question. 'Yes, I am,' he replied simply.

'You have no doubts about what happened?'

'Sneha, what happened to Natasha—I hope it doesn't happen to anyone ever. It was an unimaginable freak accident, but it is what happened. She slipped and fell and got her hand caught in a suction duct. There should've been a wire mesh covering that duct, but it had fallen off. The police and I have gone over what possibly happened that morning a million times, and they've checked all the evidence as well as the post-mortem report thoroughly.

'Also, there's no evidence that anyone else was there that morning. Recently, an acquaintance of Natasha's tried to have the case reopened—I don't want to name her, but what she did was not right. We are working very hard at coming to terms with what happened, and her attempt to reopen the case really set back our healing. It was an accident, and I wish she hadn't gone to the lake that morning, but ...' Vikram shrugged, clearly too exhausted to continue.

Silence filled the room. I felt awful about opening the wound and didn't know what to say next. 'I'm really sorry. I had to ask you that,' I mumbled quietly.

'Part of the job, eh?' Vikram said with a smile, and I felt a surge of gratitude for his kindness.

As I picked up my bag and started to leave, I reminded him about the photographs of the family he'd promised he'd send.

'Yes, for sure. I'll send them tonight,' Vikram said as he accompanied me to the door and thanked me once again for the article I was writing.

'You know, it just struck me,' he said as I stepped out into the corridor.

'What's that?' I asked.

'This incident that took place at the boys' Montessori school a few days before Natasha quit her job. One of the boys, Aarav, I think, had done something in school—refused to wear his shoes on his own or something like that—and the teacher got into a rage, called Natasha and told her what a serious issue it was. That was bullshit because they were four years old, for god's sake! But this teacher was really worked up about it, and she told Natasha the boys needed disciplining and that their mom ought to be around more. She more or less told Natasha she needed to quit her job.'

'Are you serious?'

'I told her we should change their school. But Natasha became obsessed with what the teacher had told her. It was as if someone was finally confirming the doubts she'd had all along about choosing to be a working mom.'

'And she just quit?'

'She just quit.'

I didn't have my Honda Activa with me that evening, and as I pulled out my phone to book an autorickshaw, I looked at my WhatsApp notifications. Four were the same meme my mother had sent on three different family groups as well as on private chat, just in case I'd missed seeing it on the other three groups. There was an evening plan brewing for next week on an office group that was so vague that the only way I could respond was with a thumbs up emoji. And there was a message from Smitten Samar. '*Any luck?*' he wanted to know.

I mean, *really*. Here I was, writing my big story on a loving couple, together for twenty years but torn apart by the cold hands of the Grim Reaper. Did I really have the time or headspace to deal with Stupid Samar who had been too ... too ... too stupid to ask for Aalia's number when she'd been standing right in front of him, practically throwing herself at him? Was I supposed to gather my thoughts and get started on my story or figure out a way for these two fools to get together? Aargh! I was so mad!

'*She's not interest ...,*' I started typing and then deleted the message.

Ah, fuck, I cursed internally. As I told the auto to take a left at the Anjaneya mandir, with its Hanuman statue that was twice the height of the temple, I had no choice but to text Aalia.

'*Samar from the flea market wants to get in touch with you. You can text him yourself if you're interested.*'

I sent her Samar's number and angrily switched off my screen. Between Aalia and Samar's budding romance and Natasha and Vikram's tragic one, I'd had enough. I considered checking my dating apps to see what was happening but decided to explore YouTube videos instead. I ended up watching a bunch of mukbang eating videos and was feeling decidedly mellow by the time I got home. I also made a note of mukbang and other ASMR videos as a lifestyle story idea for next week's pitch meeting. But first, Natasha.

CHAPTER 18

/Users/talwar/OneDrive – Cactus Systems/Shared/Lifestyle/June/Unedited

The Extraordinary Life of an Ordinary Woman

A few years ago, the 'I can't make everyone happy' meme was on group chats and social media feeds everywhere. It was simple, sweet and easily customizable. You start with the words 'I can't make everyone happy' and append it to a wildly popular item that everyone loves. So you had memes like 'I can't make everyone happy. I'm not curd rice' or 'I can't make everyone happy. I'm not rajma chawal.' Or the very astute 'I can't make everyone happy. I'm not a llama.'

Here's a new one you might consider should this trend come back: 'I can't make everyone happy. I'm not Natasha Babani.'

If you're not one of Natasha's 25,000 Instagram followers or 55,000 friends IRL, you may not know what this means. But if you had the opportunity to meet her, even for a few minutes, you'd understand immediately why this is so accurate. And heartbreakingly sad.

Who Was Natasha Babani?

An executive summary of Natasha's life would probably read something like this: Natasha Babani was a forty-four-year-old Bangalore woman who wore several hats, including entrepreneur, fitness enthusiast, budding social media influencer, painter, accountant, environmental activist, loving partner and the one she was most proud of—mother. But the hat collection didn't end here. She was also best friend to many, a natural leader, a neighbour everyone could rely on, at least eight people's 4 a.m. phone call, a carpool coordinator, a cheerleader, several people's guide on how to get the best anything in Bangalore, a swimming coach, an involved PTA member, a play-date overseer, a well of endless energy and good humour, and the best home-made-peanut-butter-maker ever.

Phew!

Those who knew her often marvelled at Natasha's endless energy. Was there a hidden ingredient in her famous peanut butter bars or did she know of some secret Pilates technique that she hadn't revealed to her students? How else was she able to keep up with her boisterous twin boys, conduct multiple Pilates classes a week, maintain several close relationships and remain dedicated to the cause of cleaning Lake Ahilya? Perhaps her husband, Vikram Babani, put it best. 'Natasha was driven by a deep interest in truly knowing and helping the people she loved. She was that rare being who genuinely derived more pleasure from giving rather than taking.'

This sentiment was echoed in different ways by several of her friends. Smita Dandekar, a neighbour and close friend of over twelve years, gushed about Natasha's ability to really listen. 'I mentioned in passing once how much I loved the colour teal. She held on to this little detail and got me the most beautiful teal stole for my birthday months later. What's amazing is how she remembered details like this about all her friends and family.'

Stories about Natasha's generosity and helping spirit are endless. From sending a freshly baked cake to a neighbour who'd had unexpected visitors to dropping a friend all the way to Bangalore airport early one morning when he was just not getting a taxi, Natasha touched several lives in big and small ways. But undoubtedly, her biggest contribution to society came with her stellar work on the Clean Ahilya drive.

About a year ago, Natasha Babani single-handedly organized and mobilized a team of concerned citizens, members of the scientific community and the local authorities to clean up the highly polluted Lake Ahilya. She had managed to stop the ammonia-tainted sewage water from seeping into the lake and killing the fish, and was working on having a sewage treatment plant installed. She had already organized a highly successful fundraiser towards this end and had executed several initiatives to raise awareness.

An Unexpected Tragedy

Natasha's resolve to make the world a better place was cruelly interrupted early one morning in June this year. On one of her usual early morning walks near one of the more secluded corners of Lake Ahilya, Natasha slipped and fell in the water in what can only be termed a freak accident. Her body was found a few hours later, by which time it was too late to revive her.

Natasha's death has sent shock waves through her community, neighbourhood, friends and family. People still speak of her in the present tense, as if unable to accept that she's no more.

'There was no one like her. I feel incredibly sad that she's gone but also feel blessed to have known her for so many years,' says Sana Hussain, a close friend and home baker.

Sameer Gowda, assistant professor at the Nehru Trust for Environmental Research and a core member of the Clean Ahilya drive team, expressed shock and sadness at her sudden death. 'In one year, Natasha managed to do more for Lake Ahilya than many experts have achieved in a decade. Her absence will be felt every day, but we are determined to continue her good work.'

At forty-four, Natasha died much too early. But arguably, she achieved more in these forty-four years than most people do in eighty-eight, touching the lives of countless people and contributing to improving a city she loved.

Recently, Natasha's friends put together a memorial for her that was attended by 200 people. You'd be forgiven for thinking this was an event for a beloved celebrity and not just for an ordinary woman, someone just like 'us'. Learning about her life and the impact she had has been an invaluable lesson in the power to do good that each one of us wields, no matter how small or ordinary our lives may seem.

Here's another meme that'll do her justice: 'I can't make everyone happy. I'm not Natasha Babani. But I can certainly try.'

Hi Vij and Sahil,

Have updated the shared folder with the profile on Natasha Babani. Will send it for design and publishing after your edits.

Thanks,
Sneha

CHAPTER 19

It had been four days since Aalia and I had fought. We'd mostly managed to stay out of each other's way, barring one awkward run-in in the Great Hall. She was coming out of the kitchen with a glass full of ice and Diet Coke, and I was trying to make my way in to make myself a sandwich with a newly acquired jar of peanut butter, when we found ourselves face-to-face in the narrow passage between the dining table and wall.

Both of us immediately started to back away to let the other pass and ended up on either end of the room. For a few seconds, we were at an impasse, with both of us resolutely standing our ground, determined to let the other go first. Finally, Aalia shrugged and hurried past me as quickly as she could without spilling her drink. I rolled my eyes at the ridiculousness of the scene and wondered whether our fight was even worth this kind of nonsensical behaviour. But Aalia's haughty demeanour helped me hold on to my anger and not give in to a momentary impulse to forgive and forget.

That things were uncomfortable and horrible was undoubtedly true. That I missed Aalia was also true, but it was a truth I could live with. I mean, sure, our friendship was fun, and we shared a very distinct sense of humour, but that didn't mean she had to behave like she was the only friend I could have in the world. And besides, if the last four days were anything to go by, my life was too full for me to feel Aalia's absence.

The biggest thing that had happened was, of course, the publication of my story on Natasha. It had been twelve hours since the story had dropped, and the response had been ... just fine.

I'd received thank you emails and texts from Vikram, Smita and Sana after I shared it with them. Smita had actually gushed on and on about it over WhatsApp, and while it felt a bit much, I couldn't say I hadn't enjoyed it. Sana was her usual poised self and had sent me a simple 'Thanks so much. It's beautifully written,' followed by a blue heart. Vikram sent a short email saying he and his sons had read it together and they were very grateful for this tribute to Natasha. He said I'd captured her spirit, and I told him I was glad that he approved.

Other than that, the reception had been underwhelming, to be honest. So far, the article hadn't garnered enough views or shares to make it to our website's 'Top 5 Trending' stories section, and the responses on social media had ranged from tepid to trolling. One charming person on Instagram asked us why we were wasting time writing about 'dead chicks', and another person on Twitter responded by asking if we knew of a good Pilates studio in her neighbourhood. The post about the article got a few likes and retweets, but other than that, it was pretty much dead on arrival.

My friends and family were much kinder. Jaya loved it and said she was going to share it on her social media, which was sweet but pointless—Jaya had a few hundred followers on Twitter, and her Instagram account was private. My mother called to tell me that my writing had moved her to tears, and gosh, you really could take that as a great compliment or a solid insult, couldn't you?

I spoke to Melanie, the girl who handled social media for Cactus, and she promised she'd promote it again the next day, this time with more pictures. But she also gently let me know that I should be prepared that the readership numbers would more or less remain the same.

Well, *that* was disappointing.

Turned out, writing about the untimely death of a budding influencer/environmentalist was not as lucrative as the influencer business itself.

Where had I gone wrong? Had I misjudged what people wanted? Was the world not really interested in reading about a semi-saint with ideal BMI, shiny hair and a mission to save the planet?

⁓

'Hold the lift, please!' Sahil shouted. Severe eye roll.

I reluctantly held the 'door open' button as Sahil squeezed into the lift with his massive gym bag. Sahil had taken to cycling to work and would carry a bagful of clothes that he would then change into in the office restrooms. As far as I knew, there were no showers in the office loo, and because I was always wary of him in general, and his hygiene in particular, I maintained a healthy distance from him at all times. This here then—being stuck in a lift with him just after his cycle ride—was my worst nightmare come true.

'Good ride?' I asked as the lift started its ascent.

'Huh?' said Sahil, startled by the attempt at polite conversation. 'Yeah, yeah, good ride. Best to get it in before it gets too hot.'

'So do you cycle for the exercise or …?'

'Of course. Cycling has many benefits—it's good for the environment, reduces traffic on our choked roads and is great exercise. Why?' he asked suspiciously.

'I was just asking because you cycled all the way here but took the lift instead of the stairs,' I said just as we reached our floor. 'I mean, it's just two floors.'

Before Sahil could pick his jaw up off the floor or respond to my comment, I'd already walked out of the lift and swiped my card to enter the office. I knew there would be hell to pay for this, but I didn't care. Sahil was a damn fool and just the punching bag I needed to get over my disappointment at the lackadaisical response to my big story.

―

Two hours later, a pop-up on my computer notified me that there had been some changes to the stories assigned to me. I clicked it open to find that I'd been taken off an interiors story for an edgy new travellers' hostel, a story I'd been super excited to do and that had been my suggestion in the first place. Instead, I was being sent to a mattress and pillow manufacturing unit on the outskirts of the city. This was a paid promotion that no reporter wanted to touch and could easily have been created out of the press release the manufacturer had sent us.

Oh, Sahil, you are a predictable little dickhead, aren't you?

CHAPTER 20

That Friday, Jaya invited me to a party being thrown by one of her friends from school. '*He's an idiot, but he's super rich and serves really good booze. I have the car and driver tonight. Pick you up by 9?*' she texted.

I gladly accepted as I had absolutely nothing else going on all weekend. At 9 p.m., Jaya called to ask if I could come to the end of my street—her driver was not sure if the car would be able to squeeze through the narrow street outside my apartment building. Oh? Just earlier that morning, a truck had come and dumped a mountain of cement mix three doors down from my building. And then managed to go past that mountain and the banana seller guy. So I really didn't know what she was talking about, but who was I to force someone to drive their fancy car down my narrow street? I agreed, picked up my little party purse and gamely teetered on my high heels to Jaya.

'Hey, babe, you look hot!' she gushed as I slid into the backseat beside her.

'Thanks,' I said, feeling quite pleased with myself in my cute pants and crop top. 'You look gorgeous yourself, woman.'

'Thank you, thank you!' said Jaya. 'And hello, are those *the* shoes? The ones you were wearing when you came to interview Natasha?'

'They are. But don't worry, they've been broken in and will take me through the entire evening without any trouble.'

'They better,' cause I ain't got a pair of flip-flops for you tonight, babe.' Jaya laughed raucously.

I looked at Jaya quizzically, wondering if she'd already had a couple of drinks at home before coming because why else was she being slightly obnoxious? And more than slightly loud?

'Just kidding, ya,' she said, elbowing me lightly. 'Listen, I just found out that Shaun is also going to be at the party, and I'm going to introduce you two—I think you'll like him.'

'Really?'

'Shaun was the school heart-throb in eleventh and twelfth, and unlike most of the other guys, he's still cute and in very good shape. And he's recently single. I'm so excited! This is my first attempt at matchmaking,' Jaya squealed.

'Okay, okay,' I laughed, my earlier annoyance draining away and getting replaced by her infectious energy instead. 'I shall try my best to be a worthy match for this Prince Charming.'

'Yay! Oh, Sneha, I'm so glad you're coming with me. I haven't really kept in touch with most of my classmates, and these events can be so tiresome. At least with you there, I'll have someone to share eye-rolls with.'

'These people were your friends in school, right? Why would you need to roll your eyes at them?'

'How to explain, ya? A few others and I moved out of Bangalore after school, but most of these guys remained here. They went to college here, got jobs here and have married and settled down here. They still have that provincial, small-town mentality that comes from being in one place all your life.'

'Provincial and small-town are hardly words I'd use for Bangalore,' I protested.

'I'm not saying all of them are like that, but you'll see what I mean when you meet them. Every time they get together, they start reminiscing about school and this teacher and that incident. I mean, it's been nine years since we graduated high school. Don't you have something else to talk about?'

'Hmm.'

'You know what, I'm giving you the wrong idea about them. They're fun, and some of them really know how to party. Viraj, the guy whose house this is, he's fucking nuts. Chances are he'll already be drunk by the time we get there, and then he's just super entertaining.'

'Sounds good. I'm always happy to meet new people,' I said, flashing her a smile and a thumbs up. I don't know—it just felt like the right response.

——

'Guys, this is Sneha. Sneha, this is everyone.'

'Hiiiii, Sneha!'

Jaya's classmates seemed friendly, relaxed and unpretentious. Everybody was out on Viraj's terrace, which had been built to entertain. His family used to own half of central Bangalore, Jaya had whispered into my ear, and the understated, confident aura of old money was plain to see.

Viraj himself was a warm and affable guy, whose idea of being a good host was making sure no guest was ever without a drink in their hands. Once Jaya and I were set up with some fancy gin cocktails his bartender was mixing, we started mingling with the other guests. More precisely, Jaya started mingling and I tagged along.

An hour later, I had collected recommendations for two amazing getaways a few hours from Bangalore, the name of a really good Finnish crime show that I just had to watch, three anecdotes about their old economics teacher who sounded like quite a character, two crap and one good suggestion for stories I could do for the website, and a happy little buzz from my cocktails.

Shaun, the dreamboat, had still not made an appearance. We did, however, meet someone whose name and description rang a bell—Tara, Jaya's old school friend, who worked at a PR firm. Why did that sound so familiar?

Fortunately, my curiosity was soon satisfied. As soon as Tara stepped one foot away to get herself some chips and dip, Jaya leaned in to whisper, 'She's the one who told me about Natasha's free Thailand trip.'

'Babe,' Jaya said as Tara came back, 'remember Natasha, that influencer you were working with ... for your Thai client?'

'Yes, of course!' replied Tara. 'What happened to her was so awful, na.'

'Totally,' said Jaya. 'But what happens now? How does this affect your client?'

'Luckily, she'd already fulfilled all the demands of the contract, and we got some good leads from her posts about the hotel,' Tara said. 'But it's a real pity what happened. She was quite the star of the mommy influencer world. We were planning to work with her this year on a couple of other clients as well.'

'Mommy influencer?' I asked.

'Yes, that space is very competitive but constantly growing. These influencers—their main identity is being a mom, but they usually have a shtick that sort of distinguishes them from the rest. Like a mom who's into fitness, or crafts, or mother and child fashion, or, like, funny moms. Even though there are already so many, new ones keep coming up with new angles, amassing tons of followers.'

'And this one, the one who went to Thailand, what was her shtick?' asked Jaya.

'She was more of a lifestyle influencer with a strong mom component. But one of the reasons we were keen on her was because the quality of her followers was great. I mean, she had about 20,000-odd followers on Insta, but there were hardly any fake followers and the engagement on her posts was fabulous.'

Tara and I continued chatting about the fascinating world of influencers as Jaya strolled off to use the restroom. Vegan mom, yoga mom, Sanskrit shlokas mom, make-up-free mom, organic make-up mom, natural make-up mom, pro-fitness mom, anti-body shaming mom—the list was endless, and no matter what your beliefs or subculture, there was an influencer for you.

I wondered what made a particular blogger or YouTuber break out and become an 'influencer'. Tara was of the opinion that once you picked a niche—mommy, fashion, home interiors, etc.—you needed to be consistent in posting high-quality material. 'It takes time,' she said, 'but if you persist, you will see results.'

I thought back to Natasha's Instagram page, which often linked back to her blog, and realized how much time, effort and money must've gone into creating her persona. She posted on a variety of things, from her kids and friends to her Pilates and the Lake Ahilya project, but it was always deliberately done through the lens of motherhood. Her burgeoning success in the field was no fluke. She had defined a goal for herself and had worked towards it. I wondered why she hadn't shared the extent of her success with her peers. Perhaps being the happy-go-lucky mom with no commercial agenda was part of that carefully created persona. Or perhaps she just didn't trust her friends enough to let them in on her grand plan.

～

Jaya had been gone to the restroom a long time, and I was starting to wonder what had happened. Tara had wandered off to join another bunch of friends, and just as I was deciding whether to get another drink or go looking for Jaya, I saw her waving at me frantically from a dark corner of the terrace.

'What's up?' I asked as I rushed over to her.

'Shaun's here—I've told him all about you ...' she started breathlessly.

'Oh, Jaya, why'd you do that? It's so weird when both parties have been primed, like we're meeting for an arranged marriage,' I said.

'No, no, it's going to be fine. Just be yourself. I know you guys will get along; you're very alike.'

'Like how?' I demanded.

'He's also got a chilled-out vibe, just like you. Like I can picture both of you drinking beers on a Goan beach, all relaxed, not a care in the world.'

'When have I ever said I want to drink beers on the beach without a care in the world?' I asked peevishly.

'Oh my god, don't misunderstand everything I'm saying. He's coming. Now stop khus-phussing and look happy.'

Shaun came over and Jaya made the introductions, made two minutes of small talk and then ran off on some flimsy excuse about being hungry.

Shaun and I were now trapped in the world's most uncomfortable set-up that was clearly going nowhere. For one, it was evident that Shaun had no interest in me whatsoever, and for another, when I asked him what he did, he mumbled something about e-commerce and a start-up.

In Bangalore, every other twenty-something had dreams of launching the next Amazon, and while I had nothing against start-ups, I'd had enough of this prototype of men. The Bangalore start-up launchers were the equivalent of Mumbai's struggling actors—with their big dreams and Elon Musk boy crushes. Just walk into any coffee shop and you could easily spot one staring into his laptop screen, AirPods firmly in place. I was currently more inclined towards meeting a guy who actually had a job and could pay for his share of the evening when we went out.

As our conversation grew more and more stilted, my mind was desperately working on when would be a good time to give a bathroom excuse and fuck the hell out of there. Just then, we heard loud laughter coming from near the bar. Viraj, our host, was loudly holding court amongst a bunch of friends who were hanging on to his every word.

'Shall we go see what's happening?' I said to Shaun. 'Jaya said Viraj is really entertaining in his element.'

'Yes, yes!' said Shaun with obvious relief. 'Let's go see what he's up to.'

Viraj was regaling the crowd with some long and funny story about a BBMP truck that had towed away his car. I decided I didn't need to wait for the punchline. I was done with his hilarity, and I was done with this evening. Per usual, I couldn't spot Jaya anywhere, so I went inside the house to call her and say I was getting a cab and leaving.

'Sne! Where are you?' Jaya answered.

'Inside. It's really loud on the terrace,' I said. 'Listen, I need to get home, so I'm booking a cab. But you stay and have fun with your friends—they're really sweet.'

'No, no! Hang on, don't leave so soon,' Jaya shouted over the music and laughter.

'I'm tired, ya. I've had such a long week, and I just want to go to bed ... hey!'

Jaya had walked in through the door and grabbed my waist. She might have had one or two drinks more and was in a very cheerful mood. 'Come, let's go. I'm also done for the night!' she announced.

'No, no, stay! You're meeting these guys after so long,' I said.

'Oh, please, I've done enough catching up. I'm ready to call it a night.'

'You sure?'

'I'm sure.'

'Don't take the left at the mandir. That road is narrow. Take the next left and then left again,' I directed Jaya's driver, determined to have him drop me outside my apartment this time and not at the end of the street.

'By the way, how come you were trying to set Shaun up with me? Why didn't you want to go out with him?' I asked as the car pulled to a halt outside my building, with at least two feet of spare road on either side.

'Oh, we already went out. We dated through most of class twelve and broke up towards the end,' Jaya said, her eyes half shut with sleep and booze.

'You guys dated?'

'Yep. I told you he was the high school heart-throb. But after I saw his pre-board results, I just had to dump him.' Jaya laughed.

The fuck!

'Varr-aaa-lakshmi Apartments,' Jaya slurred as she read out the name of my building. 'Cute.'

What the actual fuck!

CHAPTER 21

My mind was reeling. I was so mad, I got up off my bed to go knock on Aalia's door. Then I remembered that she and I were still not talking and went to the kitchen to get a drink of water instead. Then I remembered that we'd fought over Jaya, and since I was currently mad at Jaya, Aalia and I were both on the same side and our fight should therefore automatically be over. So I started to walk towards her room. That's when I saw a note tacked to her door. 'Gone to a client's site. Be back in a week or so.'

Aalia had gone out of town and hadn't been able to bring herself to tell me herself or even inform me via DM. *Wow.*

My rage towards her started to bubble over again. *Damn you, Aalia,* I thought. *You've gone too far this time. We're going to have words when you come back, and I'm going to move out of this stupid apartment on this skinny street that no car can get through.*

I went back to my room, mournfully shut my door, turned off the lights and lay down to think things over. What had just happened?

Here were the facts. With comments attached.

Jaya had invited me to a party. *That was nice of her.*

She'd stuck by me pretty much all evening and had introduced me to her friends, etc. *Also nice.*

She'd wanted to introduce me to a cute guy she thought was perfect for me. *Still in the territory of nice, but things were getting suspect.*

The guy had admittedly been cute but had seemed quite uninterested in me. *Everyone had a right to whom they were attracted to, but it's also true that I was looking very nice …*

Jaya and this dude had dated for nearly a year. *Whaaaaat? Why on earth would she set me up with an ex-boyfriend? Mr E-commerce Start-up Guy had probably shown up at this party, fresh off a break-up, hoping to hook up with an ex. An ex who had dumped him because he was not smart enough in school and who was now trying to set him up with me!*

Like I said before, what the fuck, Jaya?

The three gin cocktails I'd had were not conducive to this kind of complicated, analytical thinking. I closed my eyes and drifted off to sleep and dreamt of Jaya's big, fat car flying past my apartment with Shaun and Natasha in the back. When they got to my bedroom window, they stopped and knocked on the glass, and I got up and pressed a big Instagram like button placed right below my window.

—

'Babe, I feel terrible. I came off looking like a bitch last night, and I swear that's not who I am. Can you please forgive me?'

Jaya had asked me to meet her for an apology frappe (as she put it), and while we were still waiting for our frappes, the apologies had begun.

I looked at her without saying anything. I had no intention of making this easy for her. She had a lot of explaining to do, and I wasn't about to let her off the hook any time soon.

'This whole Shaun thing—I swear I didn't mean anything bad by trying to set you up. I genuinely thought you guys would hit it off—you're both cute and smart and fun,' Jaya said.

'Smart? You told me you broke up with him because he was bad in studies!' I hissed.

'I was kidding. I know, I know, it was a really bad joke, but I was drunk, and at the time, it sounded really funny in my head,' Jaya explained. 'The reason we broke up was because we were nearly eighteen and relationships don't always last when you're that age. I'd already got my offer of admission from Ohio State and Shaun was studying for his CET—we didn't want to do long-distance.'

'It seemed to me that he was hoping to get together with you last night,' I said. 'And you still pushed us together, and that was just not nice.'

'Sneha, I definitely showed poor judgement, but I'm telling you, he wasn't interested in me. I don't know what his deal was. First, the dude walks in so late, and then he behaves like he doesn't even want to be there. But I was so keen on getting you guys together that I ignored all that—I'm so sorry.'

Jaya sounded genuinely contrite, and all her explanations did add up. After all, we'd only known each other a short while, and if she was making such an effort to fix things, I suppose it showed she cared. *Everybody deserves a second chance*, I thought, deciding to accept her apology.

'Okay, I believe you. Let's just forget about last night,' I said.

Jaya jumped off her chair, leaned right over the table and caught me by surprise with a giant hug. 'You're a gem,' she said and marched off to get our frappes.

It was nice having a close friend again. We chatted about all sorts of stuff; she told me about how excited and nervous she was about leaving for her postgraduate programme, and I told her about my workplace and Vij, my super-cool editor and professional idol, and Sahil, the office moron. Neither of us brought up Aalia.

I told her how disappointed I was with the response to my profile on Natasha. I don't know why, but I'd been sure it would be the feel-good piece of the month that would go wildly viral. I had hoped it would even inspire people to join the Lake Ahilya drive. Unfortunately, none of that had happened.

Jaya listened sympathetically, which was really all she could do. 'You know,' she said, 'for a minute there, things had gotten rather interesting with the case being reopened and the wild speculation about who could've done it. Imagine if there actually had been malicious intent behind her death. People would've probably enjoyed reading about that, na? It's sad, but a bit of juicy gossip would probably have garnered more readership than such a nicely written profile about a perfectly lovely person.'

It was sad. It was also very true.

CHAPTER 22

/Users/talwar/OneDrive – Cactus Systems/Shared/Lifestyle/June/Unedited

Moms in the Wild

Gentle and nurturing, mothers personify all that is good about our species. But they also have a hidden untamed side. They protect their young with unmatched fierceness, they go to great lengths to safeguard their turf and they often move in packs or posses that can be simultaneously impressive and intimidating.

Imagine this hybrid habitat for a moment: the arid, wild jungle as we know it with the trappings of wealthy, modern-day urban life—the schools, the playgrounds, the caretakers, the parenting theories, et al. Welcome to the jungle that is motherhood.

It's afternoon and an air of calm and peaceful coexistence hangs over the savannah. Animals are either grazing or resting wherever patches of shade are available. It's the picture of beauty and harmony, a reminder of how our planet was intended to be inhabited—with enough land for everyone to live as we like, raise our young as we see fit.

But wait. There's a sudden change in the atmosphere. The air has become tense, and the animals are on high alert. It's the queen of the jungle, the lioness, who's woken from her afternoon slumber to survey her kingdom.

The Queen

Not everyone can be queen. The queen is perfect in every way. Powerful and beautiful, she exudes natural leadership that every other creature defers to. She raises her cubs with a rare ferocity and confidence, and is often mimicked by the lesser inhabitants of the forest. The watering hole she and her pride visit becomes *the* watering hole to hang out at, the bush they rest next to is the one everyone else wants, the school she sends her cubs to is the one all other mothers are clamouring for—the lioness sets the bar when it comes to child-rearing and also casually judges others on their parenting skills.

Unlike other big cats of her ilk, this lioness does not work alone and is always with her posse. Even when they're not with her, they're with her. At all times, she walks with her head held high and the assurance that in case of danger, they will gather around her in minutes to protect her and the ideals she stands for.

The Posse

The queen is picky about who makes it to her inner circle. Remember, the jungle knows no democracy, and the queen picks whom she likes without offering any explanation. That doesn't mean she lacks tact, however. Nobody is ever discarded outright or belittled—the queen understands the importance of being popular—and subtle exclusion is how disapproval is communicated. Exclusion from birthday parties, girls' nights out, group chats. But it's never obvious, and there's never a paper trail.

The posse typically comprises animals who'd like to be queen but, unfortunately, don't possess all four traits required to wear the crown—power, beauty, confidence and natural charisma. They usually possess at least two or three of these, though. Animals like the gazelle (beauty, charisma), the rhino (power, confidence), the ox (power, immense power), and the fox (beauty, charm) all find a seat at the table. And while they're not number one in the hierarchy, they're powerful in their own territories.

It's this combination of her own inherent qualities and the assets of her posse that makes the queen so powerful and hard to topple.

Who Wants to Topple the Queen?

Scratch the surface of the jungle's easy harmony and you'll find discord, resentment and jealousy simmering underneath. You'll find animals who either want what the queen has or feel contempt for her and her pack's sense of superiority.

Take the giraffes—beautiful, graceful and environmentally conscious, these animals believe in raising their young without the trappings of modern life. These moms strongly advocate no gadgets, no processed food, no fancy birthday parties and breastfeeding their young until they're no longer technically young. They want their kids to grow up in the jungles of yore, where animals and their surroundings lived in perfect accord. They're concerned about their carbon footprints and their kids growing up to be little shits who only want to eat McDonald's while playing on their iPads.

As dedicated as the giraffes are to the all-round growth of their babies, they're also terribly critical of the power-obsessed lioness and her friends. They hate their consumerist nature and not-so-secretly believe themselves to be superior to all other mothers.

But this is almost always an opinion held from afar. When things come to a head, clashes might occur, and on rare occasions, they can be deadly. But mostly, they entail an exchange of words, a shedding of tears, and after some foaming at the mouths, both parties retreat to their own turf, realizing that a full-blown war is not in anyone's interest.

Then there are the orangutans—dedicated mothers who have vowed to give their children the best childhood they could have. The orangutan is artistic and takes pride in using her talents to enrich her child's life. This includes gourmet home-cooked meals, lots of do-it-yourself arts and crafts and endless after-school activities for herself and her young.

This arty, happy, devoted mom appears truly selfless, but selflessness does not exist in this jungle. External validation is the lifeblood of the orangutan, and when she doesn't get it from the lioness, she feels slighted.

The birds—hard-working, exhausted and permanently guilty mothers. The birds in the jungle do more than just raise their fledglings. They also go out every day and bring back enough sticks, hay and mud to build a secure home for their family and grubs for their hungry little babies. The birds complain constantly about having to juggle child-rearing and work, but they also thoroughly enjoy having something else to do besides being with their kids. When a group of birds get together on a long flight, they sometimes sneer at the stay-at-home animals.

They know they're not the jungle's best moms, but they believe they're more accomplished, more knowledgeable and way more superior than the other mothers.

Then there's the lone wolf. At some point after she became a mother, the wolf decided to dedicate her entire life and self only to her children and cut herself off from the rest of the forest. She has purposely never hired help to watch her cubs and wears her dark circles and greying mane as a badge of honour. She's never seen at the watering hole with the other animals, nor does she have time to take a nap or chat with any of the other animals.

She smiles only at her cubs and is deeply invested in every aspect of their lives. Even after her cubs are older and more independent, the wolf continues on her lone journey. She doesn't know why—she just doesn't know any other way of being. While she's above having words with anyone else, the wolf secretly looks down upon the other showy animals who spend more time at lunches while their young are raised by hired help.

The Other Creatures, Great and Small

Not all animals are eyeing the throne. Some are content with their status, while several others are struggling too hard to consider taking on leadership roles.

The elephant, who keeps her calf close at all times, is above the daily politicking of the jungle and walks with her head held high and her impressive nose in the air. The elephant exclusively hangs out with her own kind and continues the parenting practices her herd has followed for generations. As long as the herd sticks together, she believes, her young will grow up just fine.

The same is true for the hard-working ants. While they may not enjoy the wealth and grandeur of the elephant, they operate on the same principles of sticking together, minding their own business and believing that the kids will grow up just fine as long as the mothers set a good example.

Not as successful at blissfully raising her young is the cuckoo. Her biggest problem is that she's bored by her kids. She says she loves them, but spending more than a couple of hours a day with them drives her crazy. Her aim is to get through the early years by outsourcing most of the child-rearing and then hang out with her kids once they're slightly older and more interesting. In brief moments of unfiltered honesty, she wonders if kids even fit the lifestyle she once aspired to. Then she takes a selfie with her babies and banishes all such thoughts from her head.

Not quite as disinterested as the cuckoo but struggling with motherhood in different ways is the black bear. She was excited about becoming a mother, but once her cubs were born, she realized she had no idea what to do with them.

She wants to be a good mother but has discovered that she has no instinct for motherhood. She's constantly struggling, looking up parenting sites, panicking, reading parenting books and crying. She looks dishevelled and harrowed, and her goal is only to get through the day so that she can fall into a deep, dreamless sleep at night.

Disputed Jungle Territory

Like in the real world, land in the jungle is also limited. While most animals have found their little colonies to survive and hunt in, there are pockets that everybody wants a piece of. And nothing is more coveted than the cub training grounds, also known as schools.

At the beginning of every academic year, bloody battles take place over who gets admitted into the top-ranked training grounds. Some animals have the natural advantage of past connections, while others have power and money to buy their kids a seat on the success train. For everyone else, it's the start of open season—kill or be killed.

Alliances are sought, favours are delivered, consultants are engaged, coffers are emptied, tears are shed—this is the first big test in a young mother's life, and she will do what needs to be done to emerge victorious.

Admission to the right training ground matters for several reasons, the actual training of the cub being the least of them. In reality, getting her cub into the right ground is a major bump up the social index, the equivalent of an exclusive club membership that offers access not just to events and amenities but also, most importantly, to a network like no other.

In a classic chicken-and-egg situation, the queen's choice of training grounds for her cubs sometimes decides the number one school of the year, and sometimes admission into the number one school decides who will be queen for the season. It's just another reminder that one can never get too comfortable on the throne, as it can be yanked out from under you in a flash.

Why the Queen Is Important

Procreation is a natural part of the jungle. What doesn't come so naturally are the skills and talent required to raise this progeny. To go beyond providing food and shelter and raise little cubs and chicks to be fully realized, outstanding citizens of the jungle who are not plagued by any of the issues their mothers had. To give them an environment that recognizes the individual abilities of each animal and doesn't expect a sloth to be a rabbit or a rabbit to be a tiger.

This requires sending them to the right school, signing them up for the right after-school activities, giving them access to the right books and taking them on farm visits once every six months (an essential break from the entitled little bubbles they live in).

The queen helps to give direction on all of the above. She throws picture-perfect birthday parties with themes like 'A day in London' or 'Jet-set-go!' But she bakes the cake herself with organic ingredients sourced from a small farmer. She discovers unknown holiday locations and plans child-centric activities that she executes effortlessly, always with the appropriate gear and outfits. The lioness and her cubs have been photographed in ski clothes as well as scuba gear. And she's also adopted a local charity she and her family donate generously to.

She sends her cubs to the best school in the jungle as well as the best ballet class, the best guitar lessons and the best football coaching. And once a year, to commemorate the cubs' birthdays, she also sends them to the aforementioned charity so that they may spend time with the underprivileged and learn what the real jungle is like.

But above all, the queen leads the motherhood race because her prowess extends beyond motherhood. She's not only a devoted and informed mother but also a paragon of fitness and beauty, the possessor of a shiny mane and Parisian scents, a talented hostess, a proud homemaker, a fun and energetic party animal, and she always has enough energy at the end of the day to give excellent blow jobs.

Not everyone can be queen. Long live the queen!

CHAPTER 23

Sahil was no longer mad at me for my dig at his elevator usage. He had approved every story I had pitched at our Monday editorial meeting, right from the ASMR videos, which I had to explain were relaxing videos that prompted an autonomous sensory meridian response (hence the acronym), to the launch of a new furniture brand created especially for young, single people who moved homes a lot.

During the meeting, he even smiled at me for no reason, which made me slightly nervous and set me wondering if he was planning to kill me. Perhaps one of his cycling friends had agreed to casually push me from my Activa in front of a moving bus. One never knew with these fitness enthusiasts. All that time spent in the sun was bound to have some effect on their frontal cortex. It explained, at least partially, why Sahil was the way he was.

Later that day, I was chatting with Melanie about our website's social media strategy and understanding what kind of posts usually performed well, when Vijaya's door opened and Sahil's head popped out.

'Sneha,' he called, 'could you come in here for a minute, please?'

'I'll catch you later,' I said to Melanie and went towards Vijaya's room, wondering what had come up. As I approached him, Sahil's creepy smile broadened into a grin and started to make me *really* nervous.

'Hi,' I said cautiously as I stepped into Vijaya's office.

'Sneha, come in,' Vijaya said. 'How are you?'

'I'm well,' I replied, feeling progressively uneasier with every passing second.

Sahil closed the door and went to stand next to Vijaya. Neither of them asked me to sit down and were looking at me like I was a petty criminal brought in front of the local havaldar.

'Sneha, Sahil found this piece titled "Moms in the Wild" on the shared drive. Did you write it?'

'Moms in the ... yes, but how did you find it? I'd saved it in my personal folder,' I mumbled.

'Nope!' said Sahil. 'It was right there in the unedited folder when I opened it this morning.'

Fuck! How could I have saved it in the wrong folder? And just how early did this loser Sahil wake up and start looking at his work for the day?

'Oh shoot, I'm sorry,' I stuttered. 'That was just something I wrote over the weekend, and I guess I saved it in the wrong folder. I'm sorry, Sahil. I didn't mean for you to waste your time reading it.'

'So then you don't want it published on the website?' Vijaya asked.

'Umm ... *published*?'

'Yeah, Sahil read it and suggested I read it, and I must say, it's a pretty good piece of satire. I think it would do well if we run it,' Vijaya said.

'You want to run that jungle-mom piece on Cactus?'

'Yup!'

'But under what category? I didn't even know we carried stuff like that.'

Vijaya smiled. 'All magazines and websites have a miscellaneous category for articles like these. So you don't have to worry about what section we'll carry it under. What's more important is for you to decide if you're okay with it being published. We realize that you probably didn't mean to write it for the magazine, and we're not going to force you to publish it. But it's funny, incisive and biting. It'll definitely do well with our readers.'

'I know you were bummed about your piece on that Babani lady not making it to our top five last week,' Sahil chimed in. 'I have a strong feeling this piece will do the trick.'

'Really?' I asked, relieved I'd not been called in to be reprimanded but also a little taken aback by their eagerness to print the article. I also really wished someone would ask me to sit but nobody did, so I continued to stand awkwardly.

'Tell me, how did you even get all these insights into all these nutty moms?' Vijaya asked.

'Well, you know, I interviewed so many people for that piece on Natasha Babani, and I sort of inadvertently ended up with all these stories about her and her friends and the cliques they have and the friendships and the rivalries ...'

'Well, you certainly put all that research to good use.' Vij smiled at me. 'Well done. Now tell me, what do you think about publishing it?'

'I ... um ... I don't know. I need a second, I think.'

My mind was reeling. I'd written 'Moms in the Wild' as a fun little piece based on a joke Jaya and I had shared when I'd first met her, of how all these moms needed to be observed and documented like exotic creatures in the wild. It was basically the result of a boring Sunday plus the realization that people really enjoyed reading gossip. I'd certainly had no intention of ever trying to get it published on the website, and that's why I found myself caught completely off guard by Vijaya's offer.

'Tell you what, let's talk this thing through and maybe we can help you reach a decision,' Vijaya said. 'First things first, why don't you sit down?'

Finally. I pulled out one of the two cherry-coloured chairs in front of her desk and sat down. Idiot Sahil came to sit next to me.

'Let's list the pros and cons of publishing the piece,' Vijaya began.

'I can start with a couple of pros,' Sahil piped up before I could say anything. 'It's funny, and I haven't seen a take like this on motherhood. Most articles on the topic make them out to be saints. And it's well-written, Sneha! It needs minor edits, but it's mostly good to go.'

Ugh! That patronizing prick was making good points.

'Now for the cons,' Vijaya said, looking at me. 'What's your biggest concern?'

'Well, it's kind of mean-spirited and was never intended for public consumption.'

'Mm-hmm,' said Vijaya, nodding and leaning back into her chair, her hands folded across her chest.

'Vij,' I pleaded, 'I don't want to be known as a gossip columnist. I mean, I've just started working, and I really want to do proper, serious journalism.'

Vijaya unfolded her arms and placed them slowly on her desk. 'Fair enough, Sneha. I'm with you.'

'I'm sorry, but I hope you understand.' I was grovelling, but I didn't know what else to do. Publishing that piece was out of the question.

'Relax, Sneha. I do understand,' Vijaya said, her face softening into a smile. 'Please don't worry about it. Get back to your work now.'

I stood up uncertainly, slightly shaken by Vijaya's abrupt dismissal. But then her offer to publish the piece had been as sudden as well. This was just Vijaya—efficient and to the point.

I pushed my chair back, mumbled my thanks and made for the door. I was just turning the doorknob when I heard Sahil's grating voice.

'You know, I might have a solution to Sneha's predicament.'

I turned around as Sahil continued speaking.

'What if we publish it as an anonymous piece? Sneha hasn't named any names in the article, and there's very little chance of linking it back to her. It's just a light-hearted take on this whole mom scene in the city. If we don't give her a byline, who could get hurt?'

'An anonymous piece? Can we do that?' I asked, looking at Vijaya. I wanted to know what she thought of this unusual, preposterous idea. I'd never seen an anonymous piece on Cactus or, frankly, any other news/content website of repute.

'Hmm ...' she said, staring intently at Sahil. 'It's not something we typically do, but, Sahil, that's not a bad idea. It's the best way of protecting Sneha here. And you're right, the piece is written in very general terms, so we're not offending anyone.'

Vijaya looked up at me. 'Sneha, I know we've thrown a lot at you, but remember that you're not being forced to do anything. I will say that this is a good piece, and it feels like a waste not to publish it. Doing it without a byline is a pretty failsafe way of protecting you, but the final decision is yours. Why don't you go back and think about it, and let me or Sahil know by tomorrow morning?'

Two hours later, I walked up to Sahil and asked him to publish the piece without a byline. I'm still not entirely sure why I took the decision I did. Was it because I was intensely flattered by how much Vijaya had liked my writing? Or because I was curious to have it go live and see if readers responded to it the way Sahil predicted they would? Or was it because I was a twenty-four-year-old reporter at her first job and deep down I felt like I never had a choice in the matter anyway?

CHAPTER 24

'Moms in the Wild' was published on Cactus on Wednesday morning and was made public at lunchtime. By 6 p.m., it was all over the website's social media platforms. Our freelance illustrator had created a cheeky sketch of a lioness standing in a children's park with a pair of oversized sunglasses perched on her head and a superior expression on her face.

Melanie, our social media coordinator, began by promoting it as a light-hearted read to help get you through hump day. By Thursday morning, it was being touted as an incisive look into the secret inner world of modern-day moms. By Thursday afternoon, Melanie's work was done. Shyla Lobo, a fitness guru and influencer, had retweeted the link with the caption 'All too familiar with this jungle! Roaring with laughter!'

No-brain Sahil had been right. The article turned out to be an absolute smasher, and my heart overflowed with joy as I obsessively refreshed the home page to see the views on the article climb their way to the top of the Top 5

Trending section. Something I had written on a whim was the most read story on our website. This was the best thing that had happened to me in my young career, and ugh, I couldn't share it with anyone. I felt a sharp pang of regret as I wondered if I should've let them carry my name. *Never mind*, I thought, giving my shoulders a little shake to shrug off the thought. What was done was done. The world may not know who was behind this, but I did. And my bosses did. And they were delighted with me. This was what a win felt like—it felt absolutely terrific.

For now, however, it was business as usual. I was packing up my bag to go check out the new furniture studio, the one with the special Gen Z range, when Melanie called out to me.

'Sneha, want to do The Distillery tonight? Myra, Khushi and Jay are also coming.'

'Hey, yes, for sure,' I replied, elated that a plan was brewing. Nobody besides Vijaya, Sahil and I knew that I'd written the article, and while I would've loved to do a celebratory drink, I wasn't ready to tell anyone from the office that I was the author just yet. A spontaneous evening out was just what I needed, and I asked Melanie to text what time to see them there.

'See you guys!' I tittered, feeling the happiest I'd felt in a really long time. The last two weeks had been so crappy, with my fight with Aalia, that bizarre party I went to with Jaya and the absolute damp squib that had been my Natasha profile. I felt like the universe was finally giving me a break, and I was ready to enjoy every minute of it.

For the proprietor and head designer of an 'edgy lifestyle brand' (their words, not mine), Aryan Kothari was the squarest individual I'd ever met. Slightly overweight and of medium height, he was wearing a white shirt tucked into black trousers that were being held up by a belt with a thin gold buckle I'd only seen men over the age of sixty wear. He had the neatly parted hair of a schoolboy whose mother dabbed on a few drops of oil and combed his hair every morning before dropping him off to the bus stop. Rectangular, rimless glasses and a timid manner completed the persona.

Aryan was showing us a desk his team had created that doubled up as a dining table. It was a neat design with concealed storage to quickly tuck away your documents and electronic devices when converting it from a desk to a dining table. It came in two sizes, and the wood polish could be customized.

'And now if you could please follow me, Miss Sneha,' Aryan said, insisting on calling me Miss Sneha. 'This is our sofa that won an award in Milan last year. It can be assembled and taken apart without any tools, and when it's boxed, you can carry it with you on a bike—it's that compact.'

As I watched his salespeople give me a demo of the magical sofa, I felt my phone vibrate in my bag. *Probably Melanie telling me they're on their way to the bar*, I thought, pulling out my phone to check.

It wasn't Melanie. It was a WhatsApp message from Smita Dandekar. I had disabled message previews on the home screen, so I couldn't tell what the message said. *I'll check it later*, I thought, clearing notifications and putting the phone back in my bag.

By the time Aryan and his team had shown me their entire range, I was quite impressed and vowed to get myself something once I'd moved out of Aalia's apartment. I couldn't *actually* afford to buy anything right now, but maybe after my 'Moms in the Wild' triumph, Vijaya would give me a raise. Else, there were always EMIs.

For now, Aryan gave me a nifty little phone/tablet stand with a built-in light for an improved video calling experience. It was no collapsible sofa, but it was pretty sleek.

I thanked Aryan and his team for a wonderful demonstration and headed towards my Activa. The office gang was meeting at The Distillery in an hour. That gave me enough time to drop my two-wheeler home, freshen up and take an auto to the pub. Say what you will about my generation, but we're responsible drinkers.

Forty-five minutes later, as I was happily seated in an autorickshaw, my phone beeped again. It was another message from Smita. It had slipped my mind to check her first message, and I opened the app to see what she was texting about.

'Did you write that moms in the wild article?'

CHAPTER 25

My heart sank to the pit of my stomach. This one had been sent nearly two hours ago and there was also the one she'd just sent.

'*Sneha, please respond. Did you write it?*'

My hands went cold, and I broke out into a light sweat. How had this happened? How had Smita made the connection so quickly? Vijaya had assured me I'd be protected.

My mind raced a mile a minute as I tried to think back to the article. Had I written anything that might have given me away? I'd been so careful to remove any references to any real incidents in the final edit. How had she figured it was me? And now that she'd asked me, how was I supposed to respond?

Just deny it. I had no other option but to point-blank say I wasn't the author. But how should I word my denial? I didn't want to sound either belligerent or defensive. My response needed to be breezy and friendly but firm.

'Hey, Smita. Just seeing your messages. Was working. Nope, I didn't write it. I have no idea who did! Nobody in the office knows.'

I stared at the screen, hoping desperately she'd buy the lie and drop the subject. My read receipts were off, and I had no blue ticks to inform me if she'd seen the message or not. Suddenly, she appeared online and the words 'Smita is typing' popped up at the top of the chat window.

Minutes ticked by as she kept typing. And I mean *literal* minutes. I'd almost reached The Distillery but Smita continued to play peek-a-boo on WhatsApp—she was either typing or disappearing completely. Still, no message came through, and my anxiety grew with every passing minute.

By the time I arrived at the pub, Smita had still not responded. I paid the auto driver and stepped out only to be immediately accosted by Jay and Khushi, who were smoking outside the pub. It was open mic night at The Distillery, and budding poets had been unburdening themselves on their hapless audience all evening. Jay and Khushi were cracking up as they told me about a young man's poem about discovering himself through masturbation. It was silly and funny and exactly the type of thing that would have normally sent me into paroxysms of laughter. Now, all I could manage was a fake smile and a completely unconvincing exclamation of 'That's *too* funny!'

'You need a drink!' Jay declared, and we all trooped inside to join Melanie and Myra, who were staring at the poet currently on stage. I slid onto a barstool next to Melanie, who poured me a beer from the pitcher they'd ordered and got me up to speed on what was happening. 'He's very worried about the planet, and he's got a nice smile, so we're indulging him.'

I took a sip of my beer and checked my phone. There was a WhatsApp notification from Smita. It was a thumbs up emoji.

The fuck! After fifteen minutes of intense typing, she finally sends me a goddamn thumbs up emoji? What kind of passive-aggressive torture technique was this?

I looked up from my phone and around at the bar filled with relaxed, happy people united by their love of cheap beer and masala papad that never went soggy, no matter how much onion, tomato, lime and green chilli you threw at it. For tonight, I needed to be that papad. I had to stay firm and not crumble, no matter what tactics Smita used to get the truth out of me.

I took another long sip of my beer and decided to take control of my disorganized thoughts.

I remembered something Aalia had taught me. She had struggled with intense anxiety in high school, and her parents had taken her to a cognitive behavioural therapist, who had helped her a lot. One technique she swore by was to think a situation through to the end and ask yourself: what is the worst that could happen? Most of the time, she said, the result was something she could accept and deal with. Just having that knowledge reduced her anxiety and allowed her to keep going.

So what was the worst-case scenario here? For Smita to slyly interrogate me about my involvement? Well, I would just keep denying it. Even if she called the office and checked, they would corroborate my story. There was no way this was getting out.

This is manageable, I told myself, and turned my attention to the poet on stage. The cute but melancholy climate activist–poet was reminding us that the planet as we know it is imploding, and here I was, stressing over some entitled lady's opinion of me. *Get some perspective here, Sneha*, I chided myself, pushing all thoughts of Smita to the farthest chambers of my mind.

Next up on stage was a software engineer/poet who took digs at his Malayali roots and software colleagues, or, as he called them, his cursed community of coders. His razor-sharp insights were hysterical, and when he did a whole bit on the hybrid Tamil-American accent his boss spoke in, none of us could keep it together. The combination of beer and a solid belly laugh put me in a fabulously mellow mood, and I completely forgot about Smita and all the other jungle animals.

'Oh, that was *raaaaack saaaalid*! I would pay *taaap daaaallar* to watch that again!' Myra was loudly mimicking the software engineer stand-up comedian as we all waited outside for our respective cabs and autos to show up.

'Ooh, yeah, the evening made major *praaagress* once that dude came on,' I replied, as I felt someone tugging at my arm. It was Melanie.

'Hey, Sneha, did you see this?' Melanie asked.

'What's that, Mel?'

'This comment on Instagram under the "Moms in the Wild" post. It says, "This article has been written by Sneha. Now we know who the snake in the jungle is,"' Melanie read out.

'Let me see that!' I said, violently jerking the phone from Melanie's hand. 'Sorry! I just ... what is this?'

The comment was right near the bottom, posted about an hour ago by someone called Trust387. I clicked on the handle, and it took me to a private account without a picture or bio. It had zero posts or followers and had obviously been created only to post this comment.

I went back to Cactus's Instagram page and saw that nobody had liked Trust387's comment. There were even a couple of comments after it, and so far, it didn't seem like it had created much of an impact. I returned the phone to Melanie, who was looking at me curiously.

'Sne, did you ... do you know who posted this?' she asked gently.

'Nope, it's some unknown private account, and I don't know why this weirdo would think it's me,' I replied, trying to sound calm and be heard over the sound of my own thumping heart.

'I mean, the web is full of trolls,' Melanie said. 'Could be anyone messing with you.'

'Yeah. Sheesh, it makes no sense, but yeah ...' I said, fumbling to form a full sentence. 'Oh, look, my auto is here. I'll catch you guys at work tomorrow.'

'Sne, you okay?' Melanie asked as I flagged the auto down and showed him my ride app to confirm that I was the right passenger.

'Yes, yes! Let's figure this out tomorrow, okay?' I said, scrambling to get inside the auto. I needed to get away from this place and these people super quick. 'Hey, by the way, Mel, can you delete the comment?'

'I'll have to run it by Sahil tomorrow. Unless it's abusive or bigoted, we usually don't delete comments.'

'Cool, cool, yeah, that makes sense. Okay, guys, thanks—this was fun! Bye!'

CHAPTER 26

Nothing was working. Neither Aalia's anxiety-reducing techniques, nor endless surfing through streaming platforms, nor my usually foolproof ASMR videos were helping me calm down. Ever since I'd gotten home, I'd compulsively checked the website's Instagram and Twitter feeds at least a hundred times, and I couldn't stop thinking about who had done this and what would happen next.

I was pretty sure Smita had posted the comment, though. I mean, it had to be, right? She had surmised that I was the author of the article, and when she couldn't get me to confess, she'd decided to stealthily attack me by leaving this anonymous comment online. What a cruel, underhanded thing to do. This was exactly the sort of sneaky plan I would expect a person like her to come up with. It was almost too obvious.

Actually, was it too obvious?

Smita was outright crass and off-putting with all her boasting about her wealth and her ugly duplex apartment. This could be the work of someone with a little more cunning, someone smoother, someone you would never expect to behave like this.

This could be the handiwork of Sana Hussain.

Fuck. *Fuck*! Why had I thought that these damn women wouldn't be smart enough to guess who had written the article? Honestly, you didn't even need to be Einstein to figure this one out. In the last couple of weeks, which other Cactus employee had been all over town exclusively interviewing mothers, making copious notes of everything they said and did? Of course they'd know it was me.

It suddenly dawned upon me that everyone knew it was me. Melanie knew. Jay knew. Anybody with half a brain cell knew. The only person who didn't know anything—how this would pan out, how it would come to bite me in the ass—was me.

I closed my eyes as tears started to roll down my cheeks. What had I done? Why had I written this, and why had I agreed to have it published? Especially so soon after the Natasha Babani profile? None of this was part of my plan to be a respected journalist. Blind items were the hallmark of trashy tabloid journalism. They were not what I did or had ever aspired to do. And they were *never* what I thought Cactus, often hailed as the ultimate example of a successful digital media magazine, would ever run.

I put my phone on silent and fell into a deep, troubled sleep. Perhaps this would all turn out to be a bad dream and when I woke up, all of it would be gone.

———

The next day, the comment was still there—only now, it also had four likes and two comments in response.

'*You think so?*' asked TalesOfTarika, a mother of two I recognized from the Whispering Willows crowd. '*If she's written this she's a real cowrd*' came from some unknown handle called i_am_sim.

I also had a bunch of DMs that needed tackling. Melanie had messaged me both last night and this morning, asking how I was. I couldn't blame her for being worried, given how I'd bolted out of The Distillery without properly saying bye or anything. '*I'll see you at work,*' I replied and dragged myself out of bed to face the crap day that lay ahead of me.

My mind was numb as I showered and picked my outfit for the day. Black jeans and a black T-shirt seemed too on the nose, so I swapped the black tee for a rust-coloured cotton shirt. It was the kind of colour and silhouette that I would never buy on my own, and I had no idea how it had made its way into my wardrobe. But it felt appropriate for today.

The numbness I'd been feeling all morning started to ebb as I entered the office, and now an all-too-familiar anxiety started to creep in. Nobody stared at me as I walked past their cubicles, and no conversations stopped midway just because I had shown up, and yet, I felt like the whole office was talking about me and my public defaming. I went by Melanie's desk and greeted her with a tight smile and a raised eyebrow. She immediately got up and walked to my desk with me.

'Babe, what's going on?' she whispered urgently.

I shrugged, not sure if I should admit to Melanie what she obviously already knew or continue the charade. 'Who knows!' I replied, quickly choosing the second option. 'Some randos on Instagram seem to have decided they want to target me, and I have no effing clue why.'

'Yup,' she said. 'At least on Insta and Twitter we can identify some of these trolls. The comments on the website are out of control.'

I felt the blood drain from my face. 'There are comments on the article on the *website*?' I asked.

'Shit, I thought you knew!' Melanie looked genuinely mortified at unwittingly being the bearer of terrible news.

I powered on the ancient laptop the company had given me and watched it slowly come to life. My phone would've been faster, but I wanted a proper big screen to slowly and fully read all the hate that seemed to have been directed at me.

'I can't imagine how this rumour that you wrote this has spread,' Melanie said sympathetically. 'Do you know someone who wants to deliberately hurt you? This is so bizarre—I've never come across anything like it.'

'No, nobody I can think of,' I mumbled. 'But you know what, thanks for telling me. I'm just going to read this now and well, let's see. I'll come and catch you in a bit.'

Melanie nodded and went back to her desk, leaving me to face the actual extent of the damage my article had done. I fired up the browser and opened Cactus's website. On the top right-hand side of the page was a stylized box with the title 'Top 5 Trending', with the illustration of a classic cactus one might find in an American desert, with five branches sticking out. Number one on the list was my story. I clicked it and took a deep breath before scrolling down to the comments section.

It wasn't quite the bloodbath I was expecting, but things were definitely very dire. After a few inconsequential 'LOL, this made me laugh' type comments, there were essentially three angry comments that had spawned off long conversation threads. The website allowed users to post anonymously, and there were no recognizable names—just handles made up of the names of furious emotions and a series of numbers.

AngryReader23 wrote: '*This article is so petty and malicious. the author dint even have the guts to write her name. what a coward!!!!*'

The comments that followed agreed with AngryReader23, and a few people vowed to stop reading this rag of a website. Some readers came to the defence of the mothers described in the article, and others pointed out that there was no job more important than motherhood and perhaps the author of this article had never had a loving mother herself and obviously needed therapy.

I rolled my eyes and moved to the next damning thread.

SD81 (Smita Dandekar?) wrote: '*Guys, I think it's public knowledge now that the author of this article is none other than some small-time reporter called Sneha talwar. She entererd our homes and lives and used the knowledge for her own petty gains. It pains me to see that this is the future of journalism in this country.*

Ah, the vitriol *really* began here. I scrolled down in horror, reading what was essentially the online equivalent of a public stoning. One commenter called me a pathetic and talentless hack who had to stoop to such depths to keep her job. Another commenter, Name&Shame, shamed me for misusing the trust the people I had interviewed had shown. Another one hoped I never became a mother because that child would be the unluckiest in the world.

I scrolled down, my emotions oscillating from extreme hurt to extreme anger. My cheeks were hot, and I could feel tears welling up, not just of sadness but also of frustration and a strong sense of self-righteous victimhood. How dare they attack me like this? I hadn't named anyone in the article. How dare they single me out?

One commenter had written me and my journalistic career off and suggested I look for a call centre job. *Oh, these snooty, entitled little shits*, I fumed. *They're not only putting me down but also belittling the thousands of hard-working people making an honest living at call centres.* Enough was enough—it was time to give them a taste of their own medicine.

I clicked the 'Reply' button below the comment and started typing out an angry put-down, when my phone rang, an unknown number on the other side.

'Hello?' I answered.

'Miss Sneha, this is Aryan Kothari from Woodpecker Designs,' came a soft voice. 'I hope I'm not calling at a bad time.'

'Umm ... no, no, not at all. Hi, Aryan, how are you?' I minimized the browser window and leaned back in my chair.

'I'm very well, thank you,' said Aryan. 'I wanted to inform you that our marketing team has created a video demo of the Danny Boy. It will be ready by Monday and we would very much like you to carry it with the write-up about our design studio on your website.'

It was taking extreme effort and all my concentration skills to follow what Aryan Kothari was yammering on about. 'Sure ... but what did you say ... the Danny Boy?' I stuttered.

'Yes, that's our award-winning collapsible sofa. We showed it to you yesterday?'

'Yes, yes,' I said, the bulb finally switching on in my head. 'Oh, you have a video? That's great! Yes, please send me the file. Send me both the MP4 and the YouTube link. Yes, yes, we should be able to carry it. Okay, bye-bye. Yes, happy weekend to you too.'

I hung up and stared at my laptop, which had now gone into screen-saver mode. Everybody around me was going about their regular day, making calls, writing copy, designing pages, selling ads, drinking coffee, making lunch plans. Meanwhile, I'd spent the last hour obsessing over anonymous comments and planning revenge statements of my own.

Aryan's call had come like a gentle hand pulling me out of the quicksand that was the world of internet trolls and anonymous commenters. Allowing myself to go in so deep had been a mistake and completely counterproductive. I needed to get a grip, figure out a smarter way to deal with this, and then get back to working on my other assignments.

I looked up to see if Sahil was at his desk. He and Vijaya were the key to solving this whole fracas. They knew what was going on, they were more experienced than me and they would certainly have a plan to help me.

Sahil was busy on a call, and I decided to be patient and wait for them to call me when they were good and ready. I had zero expectations from Sahil, who was the most deplorable human I'd ever come across, but I had complete faith in Vijaya. She was a total ball-buster and was the brains behind the existence and success of Cactus.

After years of being a journalist with several newspapers and magazines, Vijaya had launched her own digital magazine in 2007. What had started as a blog informing readers about what was going on in town had evolved into a nationwide e-magazine with its presence in six major cities. Cactus offered a mix of local news and newsmakers, finance, lifestyle, arts and entertainment, and opinions and op-eds. It was financially successful, and at a time when the fate of traditional and digital media was highly uncertain, it was consistently posting profits, hiring and growing.

Vijaya Ravindran was not only a skilled journalist who had built a formidable reputation and impressive network over years of work but also a savvy businesswoman who was not squeamish about money. Under her command, Cactus had pioneered several profitable partnerships with brands and big businesses, and a few years ago, she had also introduced a subscription model.

Vijaya firmly believed that to attract good talent, you needed to pay well. This attitude was a bit of an anomaly in the journalism world, which encouraged fair reporting and the pursuit of truth above monetary gains. My batch from journalism school had had similarly idealistic beliefs, and after graduation, a bunch of my close friends had joined newspapers and news channels where they were covering issues of national importance and updating Instagram with pictures of meals on steel thalis at dusty roadside eateries and selfies with little brown-haired, cheeky-smiled rural kids.

The day we all got placed, our group of six was celebrating at the college cafeteria, when one of my friends leaned towards me and asked if I was sure I wanted to join the Cactus. He said he'd heard it was a cut-throat place whose employees were seen as sell-outs by other 'serious' journalists. Stung by his words, I pointed out the 9 p.m.

debate shows his soon-to-be employer was notorious for and bumped him right off his high horse.

In the seven months I'd been with Cactus, I'd never once regretted my decision to work here. Right from the beginning, even while I was on probation, I'd been sent to cover a whole range of stories. In the early days, I shadowed the more senior reporters and picked up invaluable tips on how to interview people, look for new angles to a story and work with photographers, art directors and web analysts. The hours could be long, especially when we did food and interior shoots, but they were usually fun (unless Moses was involved), and there was always something to learn.

My favourite thing to do, of course, was write features. Simultaneously challenging and fulfilling, they allowed me to meet brilliant people from around the city and discover trends and phenomena that I would never have known of otherwise.

This will get sorted out, I repeated to myself. I just needed to get a coffee and a tough skin and speak to people who were wiser and more experienced than me. And also, I needed to stop reading comments on the website and social media.

By 3 p.m. that day, the exact tally of disparaging criticism against me was:

Conversation threads on the website: 7

Tweets where my name was mentioned: 2

Instagram comments and DMs about my identity: I'd lost count

I had broken my vow not to check comments within thirty minutes of making it. It was a stupid vow, I realized, and it was serving absolutely no one. Not reading comments didn't help take my mind off the kerfuffle, and after engaging in a very well-argued debate with myself, I convinced myself that real-time knowledge of public opinion was better than burying my head in the sand.

The only thing left to do now was speak with Vijaya. After waiting all morning to bump into her, I'd finally dropped her an email in the afternoon asking to speak with her when she had ten minutes to spare.

Ping! An instant message from Vijaya showed up on my screen: '*Can you come in now?*'

I got up, locked my laptop screen, double-checked to make sure my phone was on silent, yanked at my ugly orange shirt to straighten it and marched towards Vijaya's office. Jackass Sahil's desk was empty, so I assumed he was already in the office with her. Geez, did those two have to be constantly joined at the hip?

I knocked softly on the door while simultaneously turning the knob to open it. Vijaya was typing at her laptop when I popped my head in. She looked up and waved me in in her usual unceremonious way. I shut the door softly and sat next to Sahil, who was seated in his standard lapdog fashion, always either in front of or next to Vijaya.

My usual contempt of Sahil had been dialed up to pure loathing today. As one of the only three people who knew the truth about the article, I knew he had to be there, but why, oh why, couldn't he have met with a minor cycling accident and stayed at home for a week or two? It would've contributed immensely to recovering from this whole debacle.

Vijaya finished typing, lowered her laptop screen, looked directly at me and clasped her hands together. 'Well,' she said, an indulgent smile on her face, 'how's our star cub reporter and the author of our number one story doing? Flying on cloud nine, I'm sure.'

Say what now?

I stared at Vijaya and then turned to look at Sahil the toad to see if he was as taken aback by this statement as I was. Foolish move. Sahil was grinning like a Cheshire cat, infusing it with his very own oily uncle vibe.

'Er... Vij, I don't know if you've seen, but things have gotten quite messy on social media and in the comments section of the article,' I said. 'There are anonymous commenters who've named me directly, and people are dumping all over me. It's a bit of a nightmare, and I was hoping you could do something to help.'

'Sneha, Sneha, Sneha! A couple of comments don't a nightmare make,' Vijaya said dismissively. 'Come on, you've practically lived your entire life with the internet. You *know* trolls are just part of the landscape and that the only way to deal with them is to ignore them.'

'But they've *named* me,' I blustered. 'I told you before I agreed to publish this that I did not want my name associated with this piece.'

'Yes, and you *did* agree to publish it,' said Sahil.

Confused, I turned to look at Sahil, who still had a creepy grin plastered on his face. Why was he trying to divert the issue, the dumbass?

I turned back to Vijaya and said, 'Vij, it's really bothering me to see my name being dragged through the mud like this. These comments may be anonymous, but I've got WhatsApp messages from people I know accusing me of being the writer. I really think it's important the website issues some kind of denial or clarification.'

'All right, Sneha, I get that this is upsetting you right now. But if you think my twenty-five years of experience in this field are worth anything, then please do me the favour of listening to me,' Vijaya said, staring intently at me. 'This article is a big hit, and your being named is just a tiny blip on an otherwise very good day. Trust me, this will pass. By Monday, nobody will be talking about you any more. Already the comments about you are not even a fraction of shares this story is getting. If I were you, I would view this as a massive victory.'

'I mean … yes, I guess you're right,' I stammered, starting to feel uncomfortable and unsure of how to feel about this whole thing. If I believed Vijaya, I'd been agonizing over nothing for a whole night and day. A couple of damning comments were nothing in the grand scheme of things.

'So you don't think issuing a clarification that I didn't write the article is necessary?' I asked.

'Not at all, Sneha,' Vijaya replied firmly. 'By doing that, we'll just be fanning the flames when we should be letting this die out. By responding to these comments, we're only giving them credence, and that's not something I want to do at all.'

I nodded slowly. What a fool I'd been, fixating on such an inconsequential thing. By Monday, all of this would be gone.

'Now, is this what you wanted to meet me about or was there something else?' Vijaya asked.

'Nope, that's it. Thanks, Vij,' I said, getting up and leaving the room, my tail firmly tucked between my legs.

Melanie had been hovering near my desk when I came out of Vijaya's room and was by my chair the minute I sat down.

'Wanna go to the pantry and get a chai?' she asked.

'Sorry, Mel, I was planning to head home early today,' I said, starting to shut down my laptop. 'I've had a mild headache all day and it's starting to become a full-fledged migraine now.'

'You poor thing. No wonder you've been looking stressed all day,' Melanie said sympathetically.

My ancient laptop slowly saved each file I'd had open. It was a sluggish machine, and the battery now lasted only an hour before big warning signs popped up for barely a few seconds and shut the system down. I needed to see about getting a new one.

'Yeah, I think midweek beer-drinking may not suit me any more,' I said.

'Hmm,' said Melanie, trying to find a natural segue into what she really wanted to talk about, failing and then sallying forth anyway. 'You doing okay with the whole author controversy?'

'Yeah, yeah, yeah,' I said flippantly. 'Trolls be trolling, right? Can't control what anyone says on the big bad web.'

'True,' Melanie said. 'So you know, I was going over our weekly reports with the analytics guys; this article is poised to be our most-read article ever. You know it's gone mega viral, right? It's already received 100,000 page views and nearly 60,000 unique visitors.'

'*What*? Are you serious?'

'I know, it's totally bonkers,' Melanie said. 'We've never had such numbers for the entire site, leave alone on one article.'

I sat there in silence, trying to absorb the enormity of what Melanie was sharing.

'Apparently, Vij is quite giddy with excitement,' Melanie continued. 'They've been having meetings all day trying to decide how to build on its success. I'm doing a "Which Animal Are You?" poll for Twitter, and they're working on a longer quiz for the website. And get this—I've even heard talks of launching a podcast around this topic. Vij will probably head the panel, and they're going to get new guests on every episode. Can you imagine? A blind piece like this leading to all these spin-offs?'

I banged my laptop shut and stuffed it into my bag. If I left immediately, I'd be able to beat the rush-hour traffic and be home and in bed in thirty minutes. I just didn't have it in me to process all the information Melanie was throwing at me right now or figure out where I stood in the current scenario. I had a sick feeling in my stomach and I really hoped sleeping it off would make it go away.

'Wow, those are some crazy numbers, Mel. But I'm going to bounce now. See you Monday.'

—

My phone beeped as I entered my apartment. I put my helmet and keys down, took my phone out of my bag and opened Instagram while kicking off my shoes. There was a direct message from Jaya. '*Babe, going to unfollow you for a bit while this whole bloody thing blows over. I'm sure you understand. XX*'

CHAPTER 27

'Sneha. Sne, you up? *Sne!*'

I was dreaming that Aalia was trying to wake me up. It had to be a dream because not only was she not in town but also she was not talking to me. I hugged my pillow and turned over, determined to sleep through this entire saga.

'Sneha! Dude, it's like seven-thirty in the evening. Why are you sleeping at this time? *Wake up!*'

Aalia was certainly being very persistent in this dream. It even felt like she was shaking me by the shoulder. Unless ... this wasn't a dream. Was I actually being shaken awake by my ex-best friend whom I hadn't spoken to in nearly two weeks?

I opened my eyes and slowly focused. There she was, Aalia Rahaman, in the flesh, pushing her glasses up her nose and wearing a very concerned expression.

'Sne, I've been waiting for you to wake up for hours. Why are you sleeping? You *never* sleep at this time. Are you not well? I thought you'd ODed or something. Are you going to say something?'

'Aalia?' I said, still half-asleep and fully confused.

'Yes, it's Aalia, you dope! Who else would it be?'

'I … I … I … thought you were out of town.'

'Yep, but I took an earlier flight back. Don't even ask how much it cost. I was planning to come back on Sunday, but then I told my office that I just had to come back today. I told them it was absolutely imperative.' She chuckled.

'Why are you back?' I asked, sitting up and reaching out to switch on the tube light in my room. I really needed to get a new lamp.

'Well … I thought you might need me around,' she said softly.

'You saw the …'

'Yeah, I saw the comments on Instagram and on the website.'

'Oh god, Aalia,' I said, squeezing my head with both my hands. 'What have I got myself into?'

'So you *did* write that piece.' She sighed. 'I figured you had, but I was really hoping I was wrong …'

I nodded, scared to hear what she would say next. Whatever it was, I deserved it. This whole mess was my doing, and I couldn't keep sleeping to escape reality any more.

'Okay, look, why don't you get out of bed and let's get something to eat. I'm really hungry, and I can't think on an empty stomach—you know that!' Aalia said. 'Don't look so pathetic. It's not the end of the world. We'll figure this thing out.'

I looked at Aalia's face, her eyebrows frowning slightly, her nose scrunched up as she scrolled through a food ordering app. I knew that she was going to order for both of us because she knew what I liked, what I could afford—and she knew that right then, I needed someone to take this decision and not ask me to pick between oily Chinese and carb-loaded pizza. Aalia was the most beautiful person in the world, and even the godawful tube light couldn't dim her loveliness.

'Okay, done,' she declared, putting away her phone and looking at me. 'Sneha! Why are you crying? Oh no, Sne, did you not want to eat burritos? I should've asked!'

'No, no,' I sniffled. 'Burritos sound perfect right now.'

'Then what is it?' she asked worriedly.

Where to begin telling Aalia why I was crying?

I was crying because I'd had the worst, most tumultuous three days, and the rollercoaster showed no signs of stopping.

I was crying because my career seemed close to over after I'd betrayed the people who had trusted me.

I was crying because the only two people I could talk to about this had gaslighted me into thinking that I was overreacting and creating a problem where there was none.

I was crying because I was overwhelmed with love and gratitude for my best friend, who had overlooked how badly I'd treated her in the last two weeks and chosen to be by my side.

I was crying because there was finally one other person who made me feel like I was not insane in thinking that this was a big deal. Big enough to advance travel plans, make your company pay for an atrociously expensive ticket and be by your friend's side to discuss this over burritos and Coke— sorry, make that burritos and Diet Coke.

(I was also giggling while crying because I'd suddenly remembered Aalia asking me if I'd ODed after she'd been trying to wake me up for a grand total of three minutes. *Oh, Aalia, it is good to have us back!*)

In what would be an unbeaten record for us for the foreseeable future, Aalia and I talked non-stop for the next seven hours. We both apologized to each other for the way we'd behaved during our fight. As usually happens in these things, we'd both been right and we'd both been wrong. I was right that Aalia had been a little jealous of my friendship with Jaya, and Aalia was right that Jaya was not the amazing person I'd built her up to be—in fact, she was far from it.

We both deeply regretted the two weeks we'd spent not talking to one another. Aalia explained that the fight had affected her profoundly, and when she started to feel her anxiety coming back, she did what was necessary to give herself some space and protect her mental well-being. I explained that I was just a petty human being who could hold on to a grudge for no reason other than not being the first to blink. Aalia threw a napkin at me and told me not to be so hard on myself.

She told me about her blossoming romance with Samar. They'd met once for drinks, and she found him 'kinda compelling, not totally hopeless.' He was fun to talk to and he laughed at all her jokes, but most importantly, he was very cute! They'd shared a very nice kiss at the end of the evening, but then she'd had to travel and they hadn't met again.

What annoyed Aalia were the constant memes and forwards Samar kept sharing with her over Instagram. Aalia had a very refined sense of humour, and she couldn't tolerate people who shared jokes indiscriminately, without any quality control. She said that the next time they met, she would have to tell him to stop. Or else.

Since Aalia was sharing stories of her romance, I felt compelled to share one of mine, and I told her about the party from hell Jaya took me to. She let out a high-pitched 'Excuse me!' when I told her that Jaya couldn't bring her car to our gate because our street was too narrow. She got progressively more and more high-pitched and potty-mouthed as I revealed details of the evening. By the end of the narration, she was pacing around the room and shaking her head in disbelief, as if she had no words to describe how she was feeling. This was untrue—she had plenty of words.

Now that both of us were on the same side on the issue of Jaya, we tore her every action, her every word and her every text apart.

'Did you know Jaya was not a good egg right from the beginning?' I asked Aalia.

'No, of course not,' she replied. 'From what you'd told me about her, she seemed perfectly nice. She loaned you, a perfect stranger, her flip-flops. That's super nice. Who does that?'

'Then? When did you start suspecting she wasn't the Mother Teresa I was making her out to be?'

'Honestly, Sne, at first, I was just taken aback by how much you'd taken to her. I've never known you to be so impressed by someone in such a short time. I don't know why that raised my hackles, but it did. And then, when we met her at that mommy flea market thing and I heard the way she spoke about everyone, including people she was supposedly close to, I just knew that she was not to be trusted,' Aalia said.

'Hmm … yeah, I wonder what that's about, though,' I said. 'Can you imagine what she's saying about me right now?'

'Oh, I have no doubt she's bitching you out to everyone in that precious Weeping Willows of hers.' Aalia snorted derisively.

'Whispering,' I corrected her.

Aalia raised an eyebrow and looked at me. 'Hain? You think she's whispering about you to the others? Like Chinese whispers? It's possible. Highly probably, actually. It seems like her strategy, right, to spread little rumours that can't be traced back to her. She's a wily one—'

'No, no!' I started laughing as I interrupted her. 'The name of her precious building complex—it's Whispering Willows, not Weeping Willows.'

'Oh! Either way, both are equally pretentious,' said Aalia. 'Seriously, give me a Sri Varralakshmi Apartments over Whispering Willows any day. Our building's name has so much heft and meaning—do you know, I've never got the spelling right, which, I feel, speaks to its inner strength. What the fuck are even whispering willows? Sounds like a horror movie about cannibalistic trees. I would die of mortification every time I had to call and order anything for Whispering Willows. Ugh!'

I was laughing and nodding in rapid agreement at every word she was saying. Whispering Willows was a laughably pompous name but, frankly, so was Sri Varralakshmi Apartments—a narrow four-storey building with fourteen tiny apartments, no lift and a basement parking that would fit right into this horror movie Aalia was talking about. But it was proudly local, and that was saying something about it.

'By the way, I haven't shown you the final nail in the Jaya coffin,' I said, pulling out my phone and showing her Jaya's message about her decision to unfollow me. 'The minute this whole article bomb burst, guess who was the first to run?'

'Shit, Sne, she's really something!' Aalia exclaimed. 'But all in all, good riddance! As if you need her toxic energy contaminating your Instagram. Stupid, basic bitch! But listen, I do want to ask you—what about this article? Why did you write it?'

'I don't know, man.' I sighed. I'd asked myself the same question a million times. 'I was bored, and I was thinking about how a juicy, gossipy story sells so much better than a saccharine one, and I had all these notes and stories on all of Natasha's friends. I just wrote some stuff for myself and saved it in the wrong folder. That dolt Sahil saw it and showed it to Vij.'

I described that first meeting I'd had with Sahil and Vijaya in detail. I went over the hesitations I'd voiced and the solutions they'd come up with to protect me.

'Ultimately, it was my decision to publish it,' I said, shrugging. 'One of those "You made your bed, now get under the sheets and stay there till this thing passes over" situations.'

'I don't know, Sne,' Aalia said slowly. 'It really feels like you pretty much had no choice in the matter. I mean, you've been there, like, a little over six months. It's hard to say no to people so much more senior and experienced.'

I sat there without saying a word. I felt exactly the same way, but at the end of the day, I had been given a choice, and I chose to publish.

'There's another thing that's niggling at me,' Aalia continued. 'If this Vij of yours is such an experienced journalist who's been running this website for a million years, there's no chance she wouldn't have known that you'd be outed. When I think about it now, the idea of publishing it anonymously is so ludicrous that she may as well have asked you to put your name to it—at least you'd have gotten some fame and notoriety out of it.'

'Aalia, I found out today that it's going to become our most read article *ever*. They've received some staggering page views that I can't remember right now because you know me and numbers. But I know for certain that this is attracting some serious new readership to the site, and they're spinning a bunch of other stories and even a podcast around it,' I said.

As I spoke to Aalia, I started to get more and more worked up.

'You know what, Aalia. You're right. This is bullshit. I interviewed these women. I spent weeks hearing them go on and on about their precious kids and their swimming classes and their parenting styles and their schools. Oh god, the schools! You would think their children had won a Lok Sabha election, they're that proud of which school they go to. And after I write the damn thing, all I get for it is a bunch of hate, while the website starts planning a podcast. I WANT TO DO A PODCAST! YOU KNOW I LOVE PODCASTS!' I shouted, too angry to remember what to even focus my anger on.

'YES!' Aalia said with equal enthusiasm. 'YOU DO LOVE PODCASTS! You're the one who sent me that serial killer podcast, like, five years ago and have been threatening to unfriend me if I don't listen to it. And I haven't heard it, and you're still my friend because that's how awesome a person you are.'

'It's not a serial killer podcast, you nutcase—it's called *Serial*!' I said, bursting into uncontrollable laughter.

Nothing about my situation with the website or poor dead Natasha's friends had changed, but talking to Aalia made everything better. Whoever said 'communication is key' was a very astute person indeed, I thought, as Aalia and I roared with laughter over what was undoubtedly a very mediocre joke. Or was I thinking of laughter is the best medicine? Whatever the cliché, the world was full of some very wise people indeed. And Aalia and I certainly couldn't count ourselves amongst them.

CHAPTER 28

The plan was that there was no plan. Aalia and I had discussed several options in great detail, ranging from me proudly owning up to the article on social media (this would only hurt me in the future) to me bursting into Vijaya's room and demanding an apology and a raise (ha!).

At my insistence, we'd also discussed the option of Aalia wearing black from head to toe, renting a two-wheeler, riding past Sahil and pushing him in front of a moving autorickshaw. This way, he'd be quite hurt but wouldn't die. Aalia insisted this wouldn't help improve my situation at all—she was dead wrong, of course—and the only reason I let it go was because there was a high likelihood of her not being able to get away from the hit-and-run spot fast enough and then getting caught.

My job was what it was, and the power equations were what they were, which is to say Vijaya had all the power and I had none. I had to accept what had happened and move on. Vijaya was right that the comments would die out in a couple of days and that nobody except me would remember this storm in a teacup. Unless, Aalia pointed out, I became really famous in the future and trolls pulled out these old comments to disparage me. I'd deal with it when it happened, I told her.

Perhaps the only lessons I could learn for now were not to be strong-armed into agreeing to something I didn't want to do, to listen to my gut and to check where I was saving my files.

'You know,' I told Aalia over dosas and hot filter coffee the next day, 'my name being revealed is the key bummer in all this, but there's a secondary bummer as well.'

'You mean the mums and what they think of you?'

'Oh yeah, there's them. So then there's a third thing bumming me out—a tertiary bummer, if you will.'

'Yes, of course. Do go on,' Aalia said.

'Who knew Vijaya was such a ruthless, money-grabbing capitalist? She totally planned this whole thing, let me take the fall for it and is now raking in the profits. I guess it's not fair, but you expect women to be more principled, no?' I asked.

'Umm ... I work in consulting, so I'm sorry but I have no idea what that word means,' Aalia said wryly. 'But I get what you're saying. It qualifies for a tertiary bummer for sure.'

I nodded and picked up a huge scoop of coconut chutney with my dosa, dunked it in sambar and then stuffed the entire heavenly package into my mouth. Somebody in the office was planning a 'Dosas around the City' video series, and I needed to attach myself to the project pronto. After the crapfest of the past week, I felt like I deserved a couple of weeks on the road, hanging out at darshinis, eating ghee-soaked dosas and not worrying about stupid people and why they do stupid things.

Having somewhat made my peace with my work situation, the only thing niggling at me now was what Natasha's friends—the women I'd interviewed for this article—would think of me. It felt important from the point of view of professional integrity—these were my sources and when they'd agreed to speak to me, they hadn't expected to be presented in such a grotesque way.

And as much as it pained me to admit it, I hated knowing there were people out there who despised me. Aalia said I was a classic people pleaser, and I never understood why that was so wrong. Didn't people like being pleased? And therefore like the person doing said pleasing? It was a compliment as far as I was concerned. Up until now, that is, when thinking about people I barely knew was giving me serious frown lines. I wished I could fix it, but I just didn't know how.

CHAPTER 29

A fortnight had passed since Aalia and I had patched up, and life was beginning to feel normal again. I was hard at work on a series called 'Back to Bangalore', where we were profiling people from different fields and life stages who had left the city for greener pastures and had decided to come back a few years later. There were two of us reporting on the story, and it was fun to exchange notes in between interviews. Family and friends were by far the top two reasons our subjects cited for coming back. It was from reason number three onwards that things got really interesting.

One woman in her early thirties had moved to Goa in the hopes of ramping up her handmade ceramics business and enjoying her new romance with her half-Indian, half-French boyfriend. Unfortunately, the half-and-half boyfriend fell for a fully German girl and left the poor woman alone with her potter's wheel and a sun-filled seaside apartment she couldn't afford. She came back to Bangalore, wheel and all, and because she'd burnt through all her savings, she had to beg her old IT employer to take her back, which, fortunately, they did.

She showed me pictures of her little potter's corner in her beautiful Goan apartment, and my heart went out to her. To leave that sunlit seaside paradise to come back to an office on Outer Ring Road with neon lights and frigid temperatures was a modern-day tragedy. I told her I hoped she could make a go of her ceramics business and go back to Goa, this time on her own, and she immediately sold me a bowl.

Closer home, the *Moms in the Wild* podcast was taking concrete shape, and Vijaya and Sahil were going to be the primary hosts and producers. If there were ever animals who ate their young, these two were it, I thought, shaking my head in disgust. I had ideas for new animal mom categories they could add, but since nobody asked me, I just kept them to myself.

Even closer home, things between Aalia and Samar were moving along delightfully. He'd come home for dinner one night, and like good hosts, we'd proudly served him very delicious (and very cheap) Chinese takeout on our grand dining table. His guest skills were at par with our host skills, and he won our hearts by bringing a bottle of excellent gin that he'd 'borrowed' from his father. While the gin was a wonderful gesture, the real kicker was the cans of tonic water he brought along. People didn't often think of mixers, and I immediately formed a high opinion of him based on his generosity and thoughtfulness.

Samar ended up staying the night, and the next day, we took him for breakfast to our favourite darshini.

'Man, these are *good*!' Samar said, tucking into a gargantuan masala dosa three times the size of the plate it was served on. 'You guys must eat here all the time.'

'Actually, we've only recently discovered it,' I said, looking at Aalia, remembering the morning Jaya had woken me up at the crack of dawn to tell me about the police reopening Natasha's case. Natasha and what had happened to her had become a distant memory now. From her tragic death, to the pointless reopening of the case and the unnecessary speculation it had caused, to my interviews and subsequent viral piece, the whole episode had been nothing but bad news. I still didn't know who had contacted the police to reopen her case, but one thing was clear—it was not done with good intentions and everyone connected to the case had advised me to forget it and move on. Which is what I did.

I'd also vowed to move on from thinking about Natasha and Jaya and their hoity-toity friends, and I'd achieved mixed success. Natasha was gone and so was my obsession with her and her perfect life. From time to time, however, I did find myself steaming at how duplicitous Jaya had turned out to be. But rage and feelings of betrayal were better than the pangs of guilt I felt time I thought about Smita, Sana and the lot. If only I could figure out a way to fix things.

Aalia and I found ourselves telling Samar all about Natasha's death and the events that followed. It was a fascinating story, and if nothing else, this whole saga had at least given me a macabre story to tell at dinner parties for the rest of time.

Aalia ended the tale at my profile of Natasha. She was so sweet and loyal—she would go to her grave denying that I'd written the infamous moms piece that had indeed lived up to its promise of becoming the most read article on Cactus. I, on the other hand, was feeling high on ghee dosa and decided I could trust Samar.

'I actually went on to dig myself a tidy little grave by writing a pretty mean piece based on the women I'd interviewed for Natasha's profile,' I told Samar. 'It's called "Moms in the Wild"—it's become somewhat of a sensation, if I do say so myself. And you are the fourth person I'm telling about it after Aalia and my parents, and I must say, it feels pretty good to say it out loud.'

'*Okaaaay*,' said Samar. 'Please, more information. Why did you write it and not tell anyone? Why did it turn out so badly for you?'

Aalia was looking at me with that puzzled-concerned look she sometimes got. I smiled, nodded reassuringly and proceeded to tell Samar everything, starting with the file being saved in the wrong folder and the events that followed.

Midway through my narration, Samar interrupted me loudly. 'Wait a minute! My mom was telling me about this,' he said. 'She's president of that Ladies Mean Business Club, and someone had sent her the link.'

Aalia and I looked blank, and Samar explained. 'Arre, the Ladies Mean Business Club—they encourage women-led businesses? They organized the flea market we met at.'

'Oh, so that's why you were selling tickets at the reception,' Aalia said.

'Yeah, I like to help her from time to time. I'm a good boy like that,' Samar replied, flashing Aalia a charming grin. 'Anyway, I remember her telling me about this article and how all her friends were either terribly offended or terribly amused by it.'

'And which camp did your mom belong to?' I asked.

'She thought it was hilarious. She said that it was highly exaggerated for comic effect, but it was based on certain truths. Of course, she added that when she was a young mother, they were never like that and went on some rant against social media after that.'

'Well, that's nice!' I said, thrilled that someone as experienced and accomplished as the president of a club could see my article for what it was meant to be—a tongue-in-cheek piece devoid of malice.

'Have you read it?' Aalia asked Samar.

'No, I haven't, but now I'm curious,' Samar said, picking up his phone with his left hand and opening a browser window.

'I'll send you the link,' Aalia said, reaching for her phone.

'Found it! It's right there at the top of Cactus's home page—who can miss it?'

Samar started reading the article while Aalia and I stared at him. I was looking for facial clues that would signal what he thought of it. Aalia was probably simply gazing adoringly at this super-cute boy she was hooking up with.

We finished our dosas in silence as he read the whole thing. I detected a faint smile in a couple of spots as well as one or two soft snorts of laughter. When he was finally done, he put his phone down, looked at me and smiled. 'Sneha, you write really well. It's damn sarcastic and quite cruel at times, but it's extremely enjoyable. You're very talented,' he said.

'Thanks, I'm glad you liked it,' I said awkwardly.

'Sneha is a very gifted writer. I'm after her to write a book,' Aalia said, her face beaming with pride.

'Absolutely, you should,' Samar said. 'But I don't understand what the problem is. Why are you staying anonymous?'

Aalia explained how I never wanted to be associated with this sort of journalism, but then I got outed on social media and now the moms were pissed at me, and I couldn't sleep at night knowing there were two women I'd met twice in my life who didn't like me.

I stuck my tongue out at her.

'So you want these women to stop being upset at you for writing this?' Samar asked.

'I mean … I don't want them seeing me as a tabloid journalist who'll twist the truth just for a few page views, because I'm really not like that, you know,' I said.

'I get that. That's not unreasonable,' Samar said. 'Then why don't you just take your own advice?'

'Which is?'

'Befriend the queen of the jungle.'

'Befriend the queen of the jungle,' I repeated slowly.

'Yeah, you've written that the pack or the posse or whatever will follow whatever the queen does,' Samar said. 'Find the queen, get her on your side and get back into their good books.'

After weeks of fretting, somebody had *finally* come up with a good idea I could actually do something with: befriend the queen of the jungle.

When I'd started working on this story, Natasha Babani had been the undisputed queen. But the queen was now dead. So who was going to be the new queen?

CHAPTER 30

Samar's suggestion to befriend an alpha mom now consumed my mind constantly. I was sitting on the lawns of the very expensive and very stylish home of a family who had moved back to Bangalore after eight years abroad. It was in one of those housing complexes modelled to look like an American suburb—duplex homes with big lawns, no gates or fences, a two-car garage casually left open to reveal an SUV and a luxury sedan, kids wearing bicycle helmets while cycling on pristine black roads with glaringly absent garbage bins, ladies walking briskly to their five-star clubhouse and always, always, a home with a basketball hoop I'd never seen actually being used. It was a bubble within the bubble 'people like us' lived in.

The family I was interviewing was warm and charming and had neither the airs that several newly returned Indians have nor, unfortunately, that wonderfully grating Indian-American accent that the comic at The Distillery had joked about.

'We just missed India,' the wife was saying. 'I guess you don't realize how much you love something until you've been away a long time.'

'We missed our families, and I have to confess, we really, really missed our friends,' the husband chimed in, a twinkle in his eyes. 'We both grew up here, so the friends we have here, we haven't been able to find anywhere else in the world.'

'Well, to be fair, we did make some wonderful friends in Boston,' the wife said. 'But there's other stuff about India that I didn't even know I loved so much. Like the sound of cooker whistles going off in every other home in the afternoon or the feel of a towel that's been sun-dried versus one that's been in the dryer. Oh, I can't tell you how much I love a crisp towel just fresh off the line.'

We all laughed at her joy over a sun-dried towel as I glanced around surreptitiously to see where in this garden, open from all sides, they were drying their towels. I saw no way it could be done and concluded that the residents' association must provide them with a hidden garden to dry laundry.

As she went on about her love for India, I wondered how to ask her which school their children were going to go to. That and a few other strategic questions would give me a clear indication if she was jungle queen material or not.

Get a grip, Sneha! She's just come back. You need tenure to be queen.

Like I said, I was obsessed with this master plan to get back into the mothers' coterie.

I got back to office and took a BuzzFeed quiz to check if I had an obsessive personality. I didn't. Disappointed, I spent the next thirty minutes going down a rabbit hole of quizzes and was pleased to find out that the city my soul belonged to was Barcelona, that the right era for me to have lived in was 1800s England and that my soulmate's first name was Simon.

Satisfied with my results and in no mood to start writing my story, I idly opened my notepad and started flipping through my Natasha notes to see if anything sparked any ideas. That's when I saw a name that appeared only a few times but was underlined twice and even had a question attached to it—'What's the deal with Charu?'

What *was* the deal with Charu, I tried to remember furiously. I looked at my notes again and thought back to conversations where her name had come up. She was, if I remembered correctly, one of the few people in the world who didn't like Natasha. In fact, she was a well-established rival and had butted heads with Natasha on several occasions.

With Natasha no longer around, I wondered what the rest of team Natasha now felt about Charu. Had loyalties changed? Did the rivalry still persist? Or had things thawed between the Montagues and the Capulets?

I realized that unfortunately I knew precious little about this possible rival. I googled several combinations of Charu, Clearwood Academy, Bangalore, blogger, influencer and mom, but nothing useful came. Without a surname or an Instagram handle, I had nothing.

There was only one thing left to do.

I picked up my phone and fired up Instagram. Jaya was still not following me. Not to worry, I had her phone number and would boomer-style send her a WhatsApp message. All

I had to do was word it just right so that she felt compelled to respond.

I knew Aalia would disapprove, but I'd explain it to her later. For now, I only needed to type the message and tap 'Send' before I lost my nerve.

'Hey, how goes? Need your help. Do you remember Charu? She's also a Clearwood mum. Need her full name and number pls. Will tell lurid details later.'

If there was one thing Jaya couldn't resist, it was the prospect of gossip. Her greatest motivation was to find out something juicy and then be the first to share it with as many people as possible. It didn't matter who or what the gossip was about—Jaya was not a snob like that—as long as it was personal and delicious, she wanted to know.

It was why she, a smart, ambitious twenty-seven-year-old about to leave the country for higher studies, had befriended a forty-three-year-old stay-at-home mom she had absolutely nothing in common with. It was also why she had taken an interest in me after meeting me just twice. The only difference was that while Natasha, with her full life and dazzling array of interests and friends, was the source of much gossip, I, a young and naïve newcomer to the city, was the one she could impress with all her inside scoops and scandals. Natasha supplied. I consumed. Jaya was the intermediary.

In under a minute, my phone beeped. Jaya had come through.

'Babe, good to hear from you. Where have u been??

R u talking about Charu Anand? Don't have number but can find out.

Tell details already!'

In seconds, I'd found Charu Anand on Instagram, the pictures of her kids in their Clearwood uniforms proof that she was the one I sought. I had half a mind to tell Jaya to fuck off, but she had just proved her usefulness and might come in handy in future as well.

'Thanks, Jaya. Will tell more soon. Gotta run now. Bbye.'

Thrilled with my sleuthing, I settled in to go through Charu's feed and form a clearer picture of her. First things first, I understood why she might have hated Natasha at first sight. Physically, the two were polar opposites. While Natasha was tall and nymph-like, Charu appeared to max out at five feet. She had a tiny frame, a small face, really enormous eyes and looked like an anime girl come to life, except that anime girls were pretty sexy, and well, Charu Anand just looked bewildered.

Her crowning glory was her thick mane—long and voluminous and styled to within an inch of its life. While Natasha's Instagram was carefully curated to establish her as a multitalented mom with varied interests like Pilates, gardening and painting, Charu's life was projected as a mix of yoga videos, never-ending social events and pictures of her children.

There were a gazillion selfies with friends at nightclubs and fancy restaurants with hashtags like #AboutLastNight, #MyPeeps and #CocktailHour. She also seemed to have a weakness for all-girl lunches, and there were several pictures of groups of women in semicircles, arms linked around each other's waists, one leg slightly bent in front of the other, sunglasses firmly on their heads.

When she wasn't lunching or downing cocktails, Charu could be found doing complicated yoga poses. Each picture or video was accompanied by the name of the asana, which body part it benefitted and always a little anecdote connected to said asana. There was that time she was doing something called a kakasana on the banks of the Ganga in Rishikesh and a passing sadhu stopped and bowed to her. Or that other time a friend vacationing in the US had begged her to come online and demonstrate an asana at 3 a.m. because her friends wanted to see it done just right. In all her pictures and videos, her hair was styled into a blowout and cascaded quite nicely as she bent this way and that.

Then there were pictures of her daughters, usually posing in very stylish clothes while flashing the peace sign. They seemed close in age and appeared to be skilled gymnasts and dancers. Charu was clearly very proud of them. I also found one picture of her with her arms around a completely non-descript-looking man in a fitted pink tee that accentuated his man boobs. The caption below said 'My lifeline', followed by a heart emoji. It could have been her husband or her hair stylist.

Buried somewhere in the middle of her asanas, social gatherings and kids was a picture of a food bowl. It was one of those beautifully styled bowls that nobody can actually eat—four leaves of spinach, a dollop of cheese, some pink stuff, some black dots and three purple flowers. Oh, and avocado laid out like a little fan. In the post, she had announced her new food venture, Health by Charu, and it had a link to its own Instagram page.

One tap later and I was suddenly transported from colourful, bustling Bangalore to a remote town in Scandinavia. Health by Charu was a stylish, minimalist food brand designed in a very Nordic colour palette. Beige, charcoal and white had been used extensively, with only 'Charu' appearing in blue.

Her product range included ready-to-eat sweet and savoury snacks made from millets, lentils, nuts and honey. Everything was organic, vegan, gluten-free and preservative-free. The products were available at select grocery stores or online. Dutifully, I sent the page to Aalia. There was no way my conscience would allow me to order from such a place.

So good was I at forming opinions from Instagram that despite having met neither of them, I felt like I now knew both Natasha and Charu intimately and had them figured out in context of each other.

One was Pilates, the other was yoga; one was natural, the other was designed; one was spontaneous, the other was highly scheduled; one was an influencer, the other was a traditional businesswoman; one was tall, the other was not. What they had in common were strong alpha mom traits and dedicated posses. There was no way these two could live in harmony in the same jungle.

Oh, look, it was nearly time to head home. What a satisfyingly unproductive day I'd had. I had just enough time for another BuzzFeed quiz and a visit to the loo, and then I would be out. I clicked on a quiz titled 'Rate These Gen Z Trends and We'll Determine What Generation You Belong To'. Trees had tree rings and humans had BuzzFeed. These guys were the best.

Samar was coming over for dinner that evening, which was perfect because I had a lot to fill them both it on. After being severely chastised by Samar for our eating habits, we had vowed to eat home-made food at least twice a week. It was bread and egg bhurji tonight, and we sat with our plates in the Great Hall, feeling very accomplished and responsible.

'Maybe you guys could engage a dabba service,' Samar suggested right after he took a big bite of the eggs. 'It'll be much cheaper than ordering in all the time, and it's healthier too.'

'You don't like the egg bhurji?' Aalia, the chef du jour, asked sharply.

'I love it! It's yummy,' Samar said enthusiastically. 'The idea popped into my head because somebody at work was talking about it. This bhurji is fantastic.'

'I see,' said Aalia coldly.

'Guys!' I said excitedly, eager to share my findings before they officially got into a fight over egg bhurji. 'Can I please tell you about what I discovered today?'

I told them how I'd suddenly remembered Natasha's arch-rival, Charu, how I'd found her on Instagram and then learnt that she was Natasha's twin—but opposite. I left out Jaya's contribution to the discovery and went straight to the details of Charu's yoga and her beautifully designed but tragically named Health by Charu range of ready-to-eat foods.

'They're equal in every way. Wealth, accomplishments, social influence, looks—well, I think Natasha is superior in that respect, but then I'm biased—and their kids even go to the same fucking unicorn of a school,' I said excitedly. 'And they've had some public skirmishes in the past. Oh, the whole thing is just too perfect!'

Maybe it was Samar's ill-conceived and truly dreadfully timed suggestion on the dabba that caused it, but Aalia's response to my huge disclosure was beyond tepid. *Oh, Samar, does this explain why someone as cute as you was single until now? Are you one of those men who like to offer solutions and provide answers when absolutely no one asked you for them?*

'But how does this help you?' Aalia asked. 'No, no, don't get me wrong,' she added upon seeing my disappointed face. 'On its own, this Charu lady's appearance in this whole mix of mad moms is just fantastic. But how will it help you make amends with this other gang of mothers you've offended?'

I straightened my fork on my empty plate, somewhat deflated by her very valid line of questioning. The truth was that I had no idea how the existence of Charu Anand was going to help me with anything. But I also knew that knowledge was power, and who knew how this information could benefit me in the future?

We cleared the table and dumped our plates and one sad-looking frying pan into the sink. Poor Samar had actually made a good suggestion. If only the guy could work on his timing, there was hope for him yet.

An hour later, I was engrossed in a very cool graphic novel, when Aalia knocked on my door and came in.

'Hey!' I said.

'Hey,' replied Aalia and sat down heavily on my desk chair.

''Sup?' I asked.

'Nothing, ya. I just spent ten hours looking at some really shit, completely unfunny and not at all original videos, and now my brain is fried. How do people with such mediocre content become so popular?'

I smiled and shrugged. 'Samar's left?' I asked.

'Yeah, he said he had to help his mother with some new event she's planning,' Aalia said, rolling her eyes. 'Anyway, I didn't want to hang with him today. He's such a goody two shoes.'

'Because he helps his mother?'

'Ya! I mean, no. It's just that he's so, like, all about doing the right thing. And he wants others to follow his perfect lifestyle. That's just crap.'

I laughed. 'You're not making any sense, you know.'

'Come *on*! You know what I mean. He needs to eat right *and* help his mother, *and* he goes cycling on Saturday mornings. Who does that?'

'The cycling on Saturday mornings is going too far, I agree, but he has a point about our eating habits. This dabba idea isn't all bad ...'

'I know, I KNOW!' cried Aalia. 'That's the bloody problem! All his ideas are good. I need someone with a little bad in them. Like that Japanese pottery style? You know, where it breaks and they fix it with gold or something because they appreciate imperfections in a person. What's it called?'

'I have no idea,' I said, reopening my graphic novel. 'You're just being silly 'cause he didn't like our egg bhurji, which I must admit was more chopped onions than eggs. It's just as well you sent him home—can't imagine either of your breaths being very tantalizing right now.'

Aalia burst out laughing. Then she pretended to feel hurt and looked for something to throw at me. Luckily, her phone distracted her. 'Ooh! A text from Samar. If he's sent a dabbawala's number, I swear I shall end things forever. Oh, wait, what's this?'

Aalia walked to my bed and started reading Samar's message out loud. 'Consolidating list of participants for upcoming flea market,' she read. 'Look who's coming!'

She turned her phone screen towards me so I could see the attachment. It was a picture of a list of stall numbers and names, and right there, against stall eighteen, it said: 'Health by Charu, Contact: Charu Anand.'

'Well, well, well,' I said, shutting my graphic novel and putting it aside.

'Well, well, well indeed,' Aalia replied. '*Wait*! What does this mean?'

'I don't know yet, but it means something,' I said, my mind racing back to the last flea market Aalia and I had gone to. 'Do me a favour,' I said. 'Ask him to please check for another name on the list.'

'Sure,' said Aalia. 'Which one?'

'Ask him if Sana's Desserts also has a stall. The contact is Sana Hussain.'

Aalia typed out the question at top speed and within seconds, her phone made the familiar notification ding sound. 'Yup,' she said. 'Sana's at the same flea market.'

Well, well, well.

CHAPTER 31

First, I went to Radha Shanker, our food reporter, and asked what the latest trends in desserts were. She told me that desserts made out of oats (eek) were gaining popularity, and, of course, mochi was going to be everywhere this year (of course, I'd have to look up what that was). I asked if she would feature a home baker who excelled in these, and she said she might be open to it.

'What if the home baker also gives you well-produced recipe videos to go along with the story?' I added.

'That she'd make on her own dime?' asked Radha.

'Indeed,' I said.

'I'd be very interested, provided the baker gives the rights for the videos to Cactus and allows us to put our watermark on them.'

'I think she might be amenable to that,' I said, getting up. 'Let me come back to you in a couple of days.'

Second, I looked up what mochi was. It was some kind of Japanese rice cake made out of a glutinous rice mixed with sugar and cornstarch. The last I checked, all three of these ingredients had been judged worse than tobacco, heroin and smack put together, and I simply couldn't understand why their collective spawn was going to be everywhere this year. But then, what did I know about food?

Third, I checked out Sana's Instagram page. 912 followers. She was still finding her audience.

Finally, in order to be absolutely sure that I was using it right, I looked up the word 'leverage'.

Leverage verb [T] (USE). To use something that you already have in order to achieve something new or better.

That about summed it up. I picked up the phone and called Sana.

———

'Sneha?' a tentative voice answered the phone.

'Hi, Sana,' I said. 'I hope this is a good time.'

'Ummm, I was just about to head out, but tell me, what do you need?' Sana's voice was getting colder.

'I was calling regarding the upcoming flea market,' I said, my voice upbeat and fawning. 'We wanted to do a full-length feature on one of the mompreneurs, and I thought I'd check if you'd be interested.'

There was silence on the other end. Then Sana spoke, her voice still cold but less determinedly so this time. 'What do you mean "a full-length feature"?'

'Well, it would be a stand-alone article about you, unlike last time where I could only feature you as one amongst the many stalls at the flea market,' I explained. 'This would be a full-length story on you, your products, your origin story. You know, the whole package. We would even be open to carrying any recipe videos that you'd be willing to share with us.'

'Mm-hmm.'

'I mean, it's not a shoo-in yet, of course. We like to feature home chefs and bakers who are breaking the mould and trying something new. I believe mochi desserts are a major food trend, so things like that would make a very compelling story,' I continued, not at all sure if mochi desserts were even a thing.

'Oh, that's not a problem. I'm constantly experimenting with new ingredients and techniques in my kitchen,' Sana replied.

'Yeah, I thought so—that's why I thought of you,' I said cheerfully.

'Ummm, Sneha, I need some time to think about it,' said Sana, her tone having gone from polar-ice-winds freezing to Bangalore-on-a-monsoon-evening cool. 'Could you send me some more details over email, and I'll get back to you?'

I felt bad for Sana—she was so obviously torn between her rage towards me over the article that had humiliated her and her friends and her desperate need to be featured on one of the country's most popular digital platforms. But that was her dilemma, not mine, and it was now time for me to flex my muscle.

'What I've told you is pretty much it, Sana,' I said, my even voice not betraying how nervous I really was. 'Please take a day or two to think about it and let me know—I need to pitch you to Radha, our food reporter. She'll take the final call on whom we feature.'

After a deliberate, agonizing pause, I added, 'I think one of the other names on the shortlist is a food start-up called

Health by Charu, run by someone called Charu Anand. Not sure if you know her ...'

'Yeah ... okay ... give me a day, Sneha. I'll call you back tomorrow.'

She called me back that evening.

———

I was on my way to meet Sana to discuss how to pitch her to Radha, our food reporter. Fortunately, Sana was very familiar with Radha Shanker, who was considered something of a big deal in culinary circles. In an age of food bloggers and Instagrammers, her endorsement of a chef or a restaurant still carried a lot of weight. That's because Radha didn't consider herself a food critic but rather a food writer who was more interested in discovering exciting and delicious new flavours and techniques than in dissing someone's creations.

I also had a secondary agenda for my meeting with Sana. Really, it was the primary one, but she didn't know that, and I would need to be very shrewd in how I navigated through the conversation to arrive at it. I was determined to be in control of this entire operation and had given myself a little pep talk and a strong spray of a sports-strength deodorant before heading for Sana's place. But as I got closer to Whispering Willows, I felt less and less confident and found myself asking the same question that had popped up in my head several times over the last couple of months—what the hell was I doing?

Aalia was supportive of my scheme only in the way a family member is supportive of a deranged relative—she kept giving me the 'You're crazy and need help, but I'll go along with you for now if it helps to keep you temporarily sane' look. She simply couldn't understand my whole obsession with 'clearing my name', as she called it (always with the use of air quotes). 'Who cares what three ladies in their ivory towers think of you?' she would ask.

I usually answered with words like 'reputation' and 'betrayal', and she would just roll her eyes, throw up her hands resignedly and continue to indulge me in my machinations.

I was let into Sana's apartment by a smiling young woman wearing an apron. 'Please come in,' she said, 'Sana Ma'am is in the kitchen.'

I followed the young woman into the kitchen, slowing down as we went past the drawing and dining rooms to take in as much of her home as I could.

In my eight months at Cactus, I'd had the opportunity to cover and write about a fair number of dwellings of different types, but never had I come across a home like this. It was so plush and gorgeous that at one point, I just had to stop to stare.

The overall aesthetic was of a luxurious Beverly Hills home, yet somehow more modern, with some distinct oriental influences. The most arresting piece was a stunning olive green sofa that the rest of the space was designed around. It looked simultaneously big and luxurious enough for me to want to curl up in, yet too expensive to actually touch.

Every other piece of furniture and decorative art, from the side tables to the unusual lamps, was hand-picked and definitely cost more than what I paid every month in rent. The impressive feat, however, was not how expensive everything was but just how perfectly it all came together. Nothing was too overwhelming, nothing out of place and there was none of the matchy-matchy bullshit a lot of decorators went for. This home was an accomplishment in design and could easily be featured in an international design magazine.

'Hi, Sneha, come on in,' called Sana from the kitchen, forcing me to tear my gaze away from the opulent hall and remember what I'd actually come for.

'Have you met Kutty?' Sana asked, smiling at the young woman who had ushered me in. 'Her mother used to work for us, and now Kutty is my assistant. She's a very talented young baker, and the two of us are the main team behind Sana's Desserts.'

'Hi, Kutty! It's nice to meet you,' I said. 'I'm Sneha.'

'Hello, ma'am,' Kutty replied shyly as she handed me a glass of water.

I thanked Kutty and looked around the kitchen. Sana and family obviously didn't do anything by halves, and the kitchen was as luxuriously appointed as the rest of the house. The cabinets were eggshell white with a charming grey-and-white Spanish tile backsplash. The appliances, including a massive oven, were all white, and nothing looked out of place. Warm hidden lighting gave the space a lovely hue, making it the kind of kitchen that even Aalia and I might be tempted to learn cooking in.

The pièce de résistance, however, was where Sana was seated—on a bar stool by an island in the centre of the kitchen. I'd never actually seen one of these in real life and marvelled at what a thing of beauty it was.

'Well, Kutty and I have been playing with a few ideas, and I thought we'd get started straight away,' Sana said. 'You want to grab a stool?'

'Yes, for sure,' I said, sliding onto a stool next to Sana. 'This kitchen is beautiful, Sana!'

She smiled. 'Thanks. Our family spends a lot of time here; I use them as guinea pigs for my recipes all the time. Now, I tried a couple of mochi recipes, and I think I've got the perfect one to demonstrate. I've modified it to make it healthier than the original recipe, and it tastes just as good,' Sana said, switching on the iPad lying on the island to show me what she'd found.

I pulled out my notebook and settled in to listen to Sana's pitch for a mochi ice cream. She told me how she had worried the ingredients may be hard to source, but she'd eventually easily found them at a local speciality store and was happy to share online links to them as well.

Like an eager student going that extra mile to impress their teacher, Sana had come up with other ideas to pitch to Radha as well, like black buttercream frosting and some very interesting-sounding sweet-and-savoury desserts.

I took notes diligently and asked her if she was open to sharing recipe videos with us. I made it clear that we didn't have the budget to film them right now, and she was quick to reassure me that it was no problem. She had a guy who helped her with videos for her YouTube and Instagram anyway.

By the end of the hour, we had a solid proposal to take to Radha, and I was feeling confident I would be able to sell this.

'Shall we taste some of the new items now?' she asked me, smiling, and then gestured to Kutty, who disappeared through a door leading into what must have been the pantry or a storeroom.

'Is that a pantry back there?' I asked.

'Oh, that's another kitchen for the staff to use,' Sana answered, offering no further explanations.

'I see,' I said, trying to process this new information without showing it on my face. 'Well, what you're proposing sounds really good, Sana. I hope Radha goes for it. I don't know if you know Charu Anand, but her products are already packaged and available in the market, so that gives her a slight edge.'

'Oh, I know Charu,' said Sana, her voice as soft and posh as always. 'She's a very popular yoga teacher. I've attended her classes—she's very good.'

'Ah, I see. Have you tried her ready-to-eat foods?' I asked.

'You know, I haven't,' replied Sana. 'From what I know of her, I think she's a better yoga teacher than a chef.' With a phoney laugh, she added, 'Well, at least we know for certain that she is a yoga teacher!'

'Oh, you mean she hasn't actually experimented and created these recipes herself?' I asked. 'Her website and social media pages claim that she has.'

'Yeah, well,' Sana said. 'I guess a compelling backstory makes for good marketing.'

'Hmm,' I said. 'I guess we'll know one way or the other when we taste what she makes.'

'Oh, good, Kutty has brought the goodies,' Sana said as Kutty came in from the *second* kitchen, bearing a massive tray laden with food. 'First, try the mochi ice cream. Then, try this savoury cheesecake—it has an ingredient I bet you'll never be able to guess.'

The ice cream was unusual and mild but tasty. I'd take a chocolate sundae over this any day, but perhaps my palate just needed to get more sophisticated. The savoury cheesecake was not at all what I had expected, but once my brain registered that it was more of a savoury than a classic cheesecake, I started to hate it a little less.

'Umm ... Sana,' I said, super aware that this meeting was almost done and that I still had to get to the point, 'I don't know if you read that satirical article about mothers on Cactus last month.'

'I've read it,' said Sana, putting a tiny spoonful of the confusing cheesecake into her mouth. The secret ingredient was zucchini, by the way, which should've been neither a secret nor an ingredient, in my opinion.

'I wanted to say that I didn't write it. I need you to know that, and I would appreciate it if you could tell Smita as well. She got really mad at me, and well, I didn't deserve that.'

'We all thought it was you, Sneha,' Sana finally said after a long pause. 'You'd spent so much time talking to us, and that article seemed to be taking potshots at all of us.'

'Yes, but there are other writers in the world, you know.' I was speaking fast and I felt like my cheeks were on fire. This was the most uncomfortable conversation of my life. 'I don't know who wrote it, but it could well be a mom herself. And I didn't appreciate being cursed at like that on a public platform.'

Sana sighed and then went quiet for several seconds, as if carefully trying to decide what to say next. 'I believe you, Sneha,' she finally said. 'If you say you didn't write it, you didn't write it. But Smita is her own person, and I can't decide on her behalf.'

'Yeah, but she's your friend, and I think you can inform her about the truth,' I said, getting off the barstool and grabbing my bag. 'Thanks so much for putting this together. I should be getting back to the office now—I need to run all this by Radha.'

Sana walked me to the front door and said goodbye and that she hoped to hear from me soon.

'Bye, Sana,' I said. 'I hope to hear from you and Smita soon as well.'

CHAPTER 32

'You did *not* say that!'

Aalia was squealing and so was I. We were in our drawing room, on our lone brown sofa that had come with the apartment, and I'd just spent the last twenty minutes giving her a detailed account of my meeting with Sana.

'What did she say? She must've died!' Aalia exclaimed.

'I don't know. I was halfway out of the door when I said this, and I walked quickly to the lift and got the hell out of there,' I said. 'My god, Aalia, I thought I was going to collapse after I made that last statement. Like, I was actually shaking. I had to sit on one of their benches downstairs and steady my nerves.'

'I can just imagine, Sneha. But how did you even come up with such a line? You can never think of a good comeback line at the right time. That's your thing!'

'I know! I'm as surprised as you are,' I said, nodding in agreement. 'I think all this plotting and manipulating and lying is really improving my spontaneous comeback skills.'

'Hey! Lying is bad, but I'll support whatever it takes for you to get what you need from these women and close this chapter,' Aalia said.

'Thanks, Aalia. I'm also sick of this shit, and I promise you that one way or another, I'm done with this saga. Whether Smita reaches out to me or not, I've already pitched Sana to Radha, and I'm going let her take a call on this. It feels really rotten to be holding Sana hostage because of Smita.'

Aalia leaned over to give me a hug. I knew it had been hard for her to go along with everything I'd been doing recently—which had been nothing but a series of bad decisions and lies. Aalia was the best person I knew, genuinely good and loyal to a fault, and it pained me that her loyalty had been tested like this. But she'd put her opinions of my behaviour aside and supported me unflinchingly, and I loved her more than ever for that.

Of course, until a few weeks ago, I was also one of the best people I knew. But after my sickening behaviour earlier that day at Sana's house, my opinion of my own character had gone down several notches. I felt like I'd become a little savvier, though, and I guess there was something to be said for that.

⁓

Early the next morning, I received a WhatsApp from Smita Dandekar.

'Found out from Sana that you weren't the author of that vile moms piece. Glad to know that as both Sana and I really like u.

Hope I din't hurt u with any of my comments. I'm gonna delete them. Take care and see u soon.'

CHAPTER 33

Three weeks later, right before the next flea market was due to take place, Cactus dropped a big profile on Sana. It featured a 500-word interview, two original recipes and two accompanying videos that had been filmed in her own kitchen—the pretty one, not the one used by the staff.

What was not to love? Beautiful food being prepared by a charming host in a dream kitchen—the videos were a hit, and Melanie had more than enough enticing screenshots for her social media campaign. Sana's star was rising, and her daily doubling Instagram numbers were proof of it.

On the day of the Village Bazaar, the fancy flea market for mompreneurs, Samar took Aalia and me around as his special guests, which essentially meant that we didn't have to pay an entry fee and got free coconut water drinks at the entrance. Samar and Aalia were still going strong, and Samar had tried to suggest their meeting his mother at the event, but Aalia had quickly shut that line of discussion down.

As we approached Ye Olde Tavern, we saw that Sana's Desserts had been given the biggest stall in the centre, closest to the chairs and tables. A big crowd was thronging her stall, and I went around them to try and catch her eye and say hi. She and Kutty looked a little overwhelmed with all the customers but mostly delighted with the response they were getting. *I'll say hi later*, I thought, and turned to come back to Samar and Aalia.

That's when I saw the words on the stall banner Sana had got specially designed: 'Sana's Desserts. Featured on Cactus as one of the top home bakers in Bangalore.'

The queen is dead. Long live the queen!

EPILOGUE

One year later ...

Vijaya is on her way to becoming a media heavyweight and was recently invited as a keynote speaker at an 'Ethics in Media' conference in Switzerland. Over the last year, she's also turned down two offers to buy the website.

Sahil keeps finding new ways of being annoying. The latest is his embracing a keto diet and his publicly renouncing carbohydrates. Every time he passes my desk and sees a Coke can or a biscuit packet on my desk, he chants, 'Sugar is the dev-il!' I now fantasize about a sack of sugar falling off a truck and crushing him while he's riding his cycle.

Aalia has been assigned a new client at her consulting job. He's a total nightmare, and we have spent several evenings on our brown couch tearing him to bits. She claims he called her thirty-six times one afternoon when she was in a meeting and her phone was on silent. I checked her phone. He'd called her twice.

Samar and Aalia are still dating, and she's even met his mother. According to Aalia, it was a total disaster. According to Samar, it went very well.

He also took her cycling one Saturday morning. According to Aalia, it was a total disaster. According to Samar, it was the worst thing he'd ever been through, including his gallbladder surgery.

Sana is in the league of big-time influencers now. She's confided to me that a streaming platform reached out to her to host a baking show. She is considering it.

She and Smita have become quite the power pair and host quarterly webinars titled 'Parenting, the IB Way'. They charge Rs 3,000 per attendee and are always sold out.

Jaya sent me a goodbye text just before leaving for the US, but I didn't bother responding. I don't follow her on any social media any more but sometimes, on an exceptionally slow day, I have been guilty of checking out her Twitter feed. She seems well.

I'm still at Cactus, still loving what I do and passionately hating Sahil. I've learnt a lot in the past year, mostly around becoming more assertive and developing a skill for packaging important stories that deserve an audience. I enjoy my job, have a nice circle of friends and possess a very nice lamp I got at Samar's mother's flea market. My only regret from the last year is that I never got to give Jaya her comeuppance. Other than that, I feel good and in control, and more than a little satisfied with the role I played in crowning a new queen of the jungle.

Also, I'm happy to report all of my interview subjects are alive and well.

ACKNOWLEDGEMENTS

Ugh, it pains me to do this in writing and have it recorded for posterity, but here are the facts. I could not have written this book without my wonderful, funny, still handsome and super-supportive husband, Vishay. You were/are my parent in crime, my accountability buddy, my ruse to get me out of the house so I can write and the first person I trusted to read this book. Thank you for believing in me and watching TV on mute while I typed away in the late hours of the night. Since you have no plans of writing a book and acknowledging me in print, you may return these compliments in the form of a luxury holiday.

Thank you to my kids—the best kids in the world—Avi and Zoya, for taking me on this fantastic rollercoaster ride called motherhood. We might feel like throwing up sometimes, but we always have fun, and the pictures are worth the price of admission alone.

Thank you to my parents—Shiv and Vijaylakshmi—who surrounded me with books as a child and taught me the art of being able to laugh at all of life's absurdities. A love for reading and a sense of humour—possibly two of the most important tools one needs to get through life.

Thank you to my in-laws—MP and Kiran—for being loving, supportive and always proud of me, book or no book.

I'd like to thank Swati Chopra, the first person I reached out to after I had the draft ready. And Swati Daftuar, my editor and the person into whose ears I screamed for joy after she told me HarperCollins India was sending me a contract. And whose ears I further chewed over the next few months of editing. And thank you to Siya Jacob, future celebrity artist and fantastic collaborator.

I have to acknowledge Gayatri Das Sharma, who helped me get out of my head, create a schedule and put this story down on paper.

Finally, a big hug and thank you to Sreya, Meghana, Shefali, Neha and Preeti—you girls are my forever posse. Thank you for being my sounding boards, my partners in being able to discuss the minutest details of my life, and for always sending the best Instagram shopping recommendations.

ABOUT THE AUTHOR

Nidhi Raichand often suspects that her life is secretly a sitcom. Set in Bangalore, the main cast includes Nidhi as the cool-headed, witty and lovable mom of two, working a corporate job while also trying to pursue her literary dreams. Her husband is played by Vishay, who is also very cool (not as cool as her, of course) and is often the cause of many of the show's hijinks. Two beautiful and spirited children round out the cast and ensure there's never a dull moment. Recurring characters include lots of friends and family, office colleagues and an ever-rotating cast of cooks. All this against the backdrop of the beautiful skies and the not-so-beautiful roads of the city.

When not dealing with the crisis of the day, Nidhi enjoys reading, watching '90s shows and movies, travelling and long walks while listening to podcasts. Her catchphrase is 'Oh fish!' (this is a family-friendly sitcom, after all).

30 Years *of*

HarperCollins *Publishers* India

At HarperCollins, we believe in telling the best stories and finding the widest possible readership for our books in every format possible. We started publishing 30 years ago; a great deal has changed since then, but what has remained constant is the passion with which our authors write their books, the love with which readers receive them, and the sheer joy and excitement that we as publishers feel in being a part of the publishing process.

Over the years, we've had the pleasure of publishing some of the finest writing from the subcontinent and around the world, and some of the biggest bestsellers in India's publishing history. Our books and authors have won a phenomenal range of awards, and we ourselves have been named Publisher of the Year the greatest number of times. But nothing has meant more to us than the fact that millions of people have read the books we published, and somewhere, a book of ours might have made a difference.

As we step into our fourth decade, we go back to that one word – a word which has been a driving force for us all these years.

Read.

     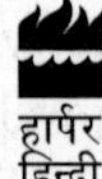